THE HORRIBLE

Room For One More

by Dik Browne

TOR

A TOM DOHERTY ASSOCIATES BOOK
NEW YORK

This is a work of fiction. All the characters and events portrayed in this book are fictitious, and any resemblance to real people or events is purely coincidental.

HAGAR THE HORRIBLE: ROOM FOR ONE MORE

A Tor Book
Published by Tom Doherty Associates, Inc.
49 West 24th Street
New York, N.Y. 10010

ISBN: 0-812-51437-8

First Tor printing: August 1984

Printed in the United States of America

0 9 8 7 6 5 4 3

MAN'S BEST FRIENDS

NOTHING LIKE A WARM BED ON A COLD NIGHT
VOOF?

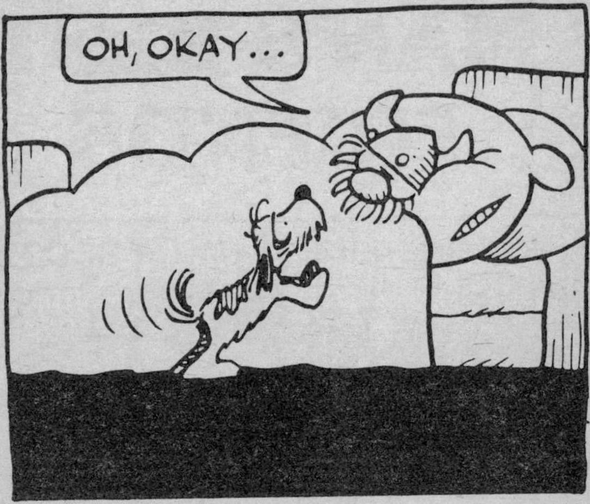
OH, OKAY...

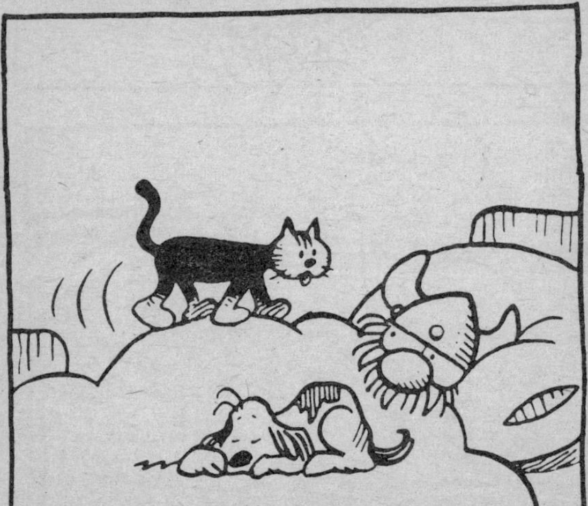

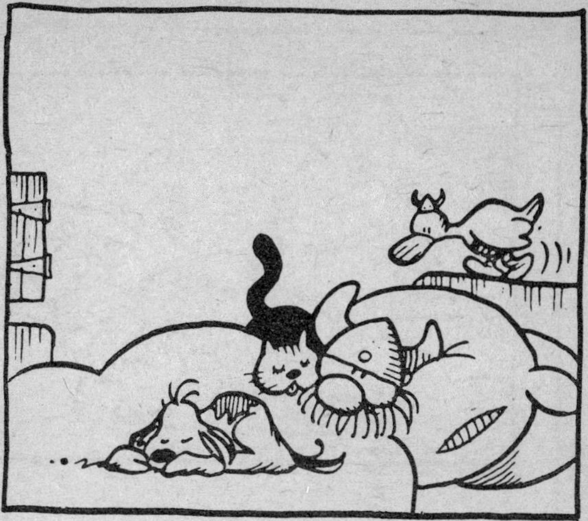

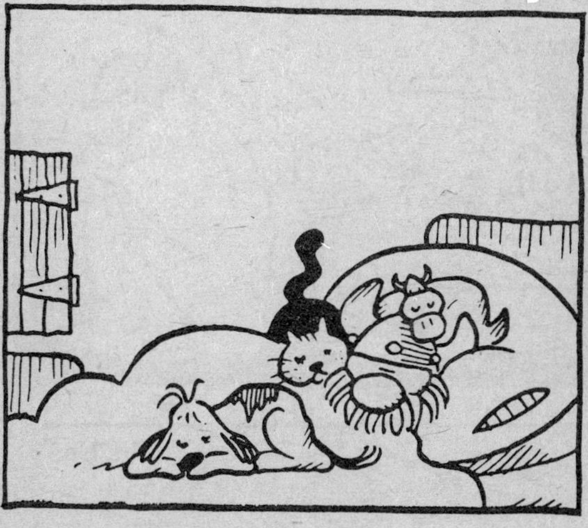

© King Features Syndicate, Inc., 1979 World rights reserved
1-14

The End

SCOTTISH OPEN

MAMA! DADDY IS IN A STRANGE FRENZY!
SIGH THAT, MY DAUGHTER, IS THE 'SCOTTISH CURSE'

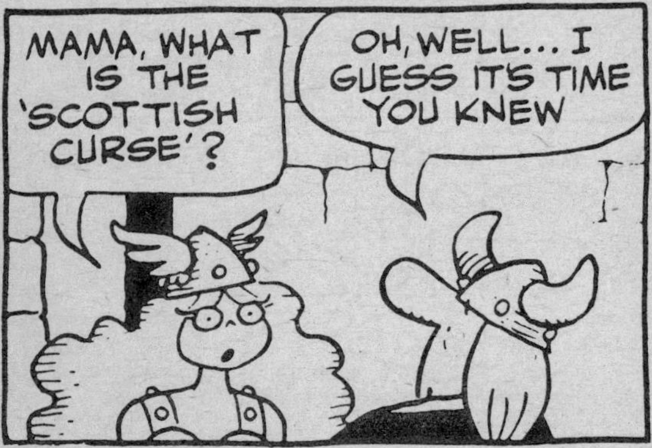
MAMA, WHAT IS THE 'SCOTTISH CURSE'?
OH, WELL... I GUESS IT'S TIME YOU KNEW

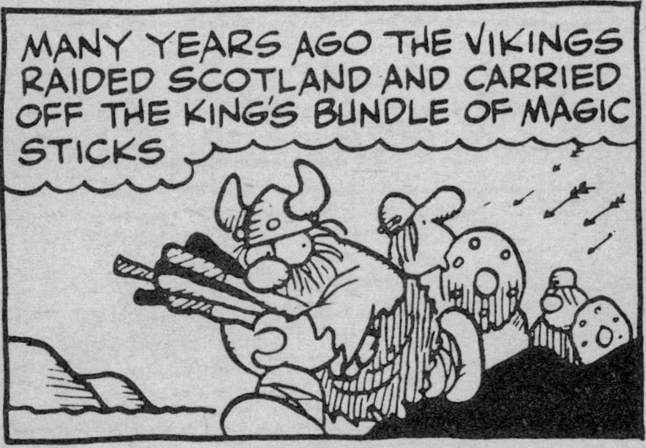
MANY YEARS AGO THE VIKINGS RAIDED SCOTLAND AND CARRIED OFF THE KING'S BUNDLE OF MAGIC STICKS

AND KING MacDUFF PUT A GREAT AND TERRIBLE CURSE ON THE STICKS THAT NO MAN WOULD FIND JOY IN THEM

AND THAT CURSE HAS LASTED TO THIS VERY DAY

AND THAT'S THE 'SCOTTISH CURSE'?

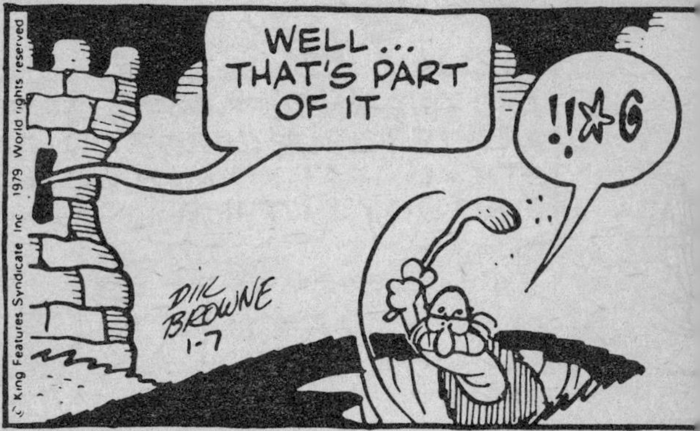
© King Features Syndicate Inc 1979 World rights reserved
WELL ... THAT'S PART OF IT
!!☆G
DIK BROWNE 1-7

LIES!

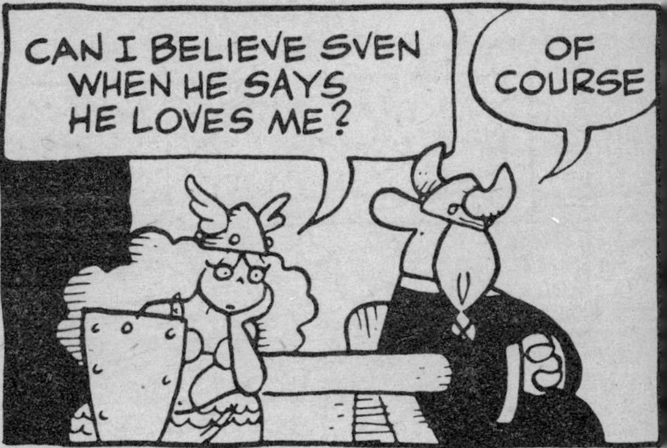
CAN I BELIEVE SVEN WHEN HE SAYS HE LOVES ME?
OF COURSE

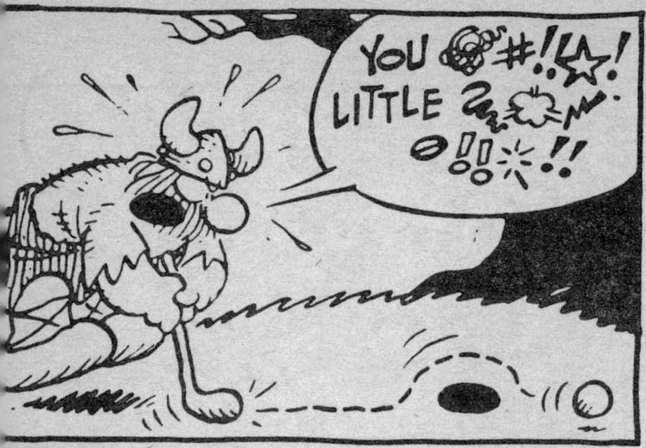
YOU @#!!☆!
LITTLE ?
!!!!

The End

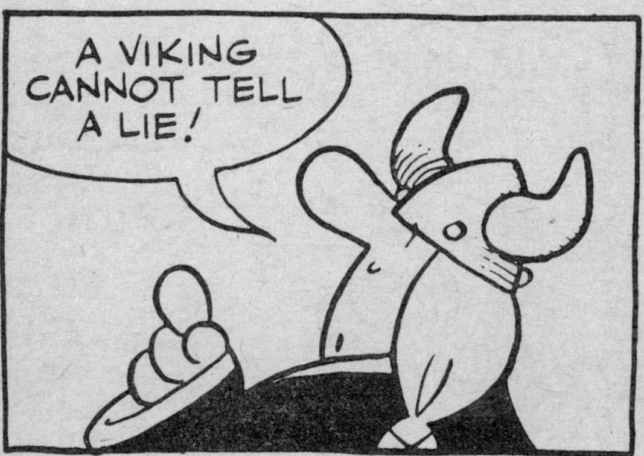
A VIKING CANNOT TELL A LIE!

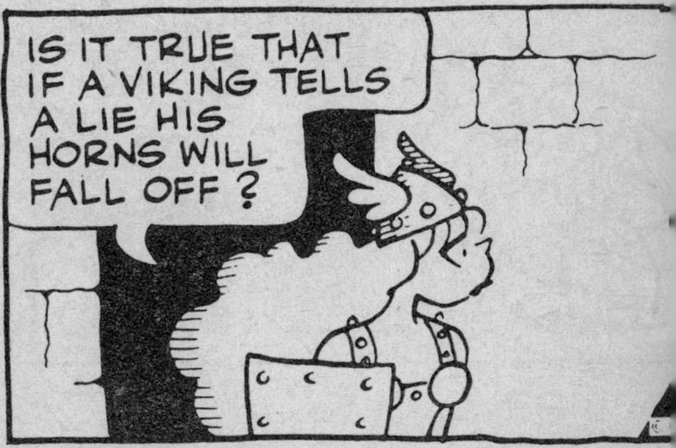
IS IT TRUE THAT IF A VIKING TELLS A LIE HIS HORNS WILL FALL OFF ?

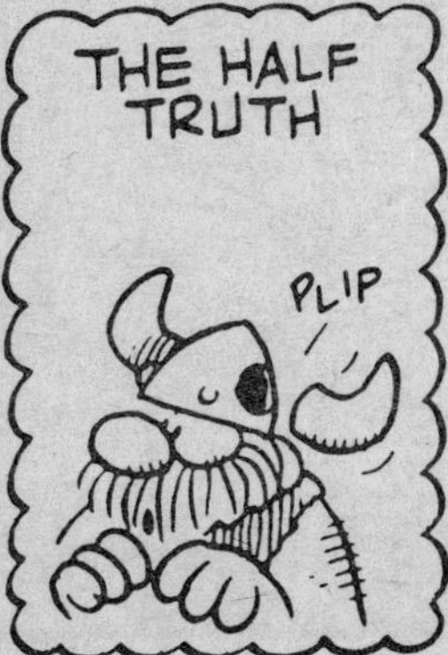
THE HALF TRUTH
PLIP

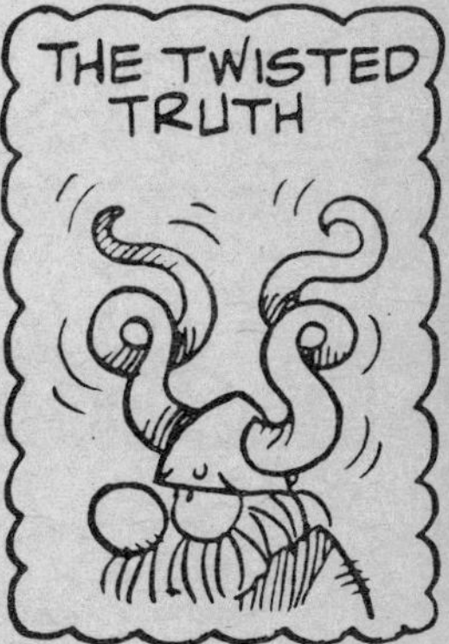
THE TWISTED TRUTH

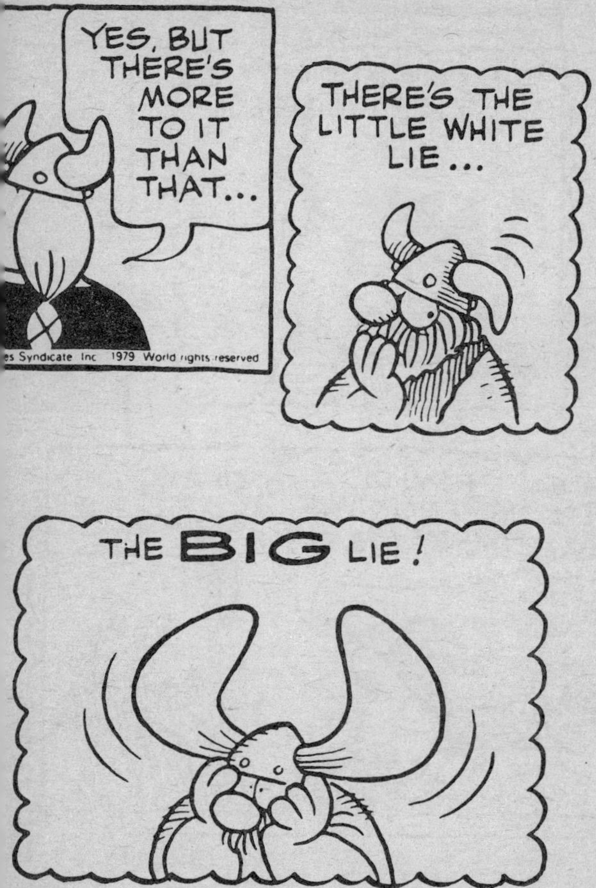
YES, BUT THERE'S MORE TO IT THAN THAT...
es Syndicate Inc 1979 World rights reserved
THERE'S THE LITTLE WHITE LIE...
THE BIG LIE!

THE OUT-AND-OUT BRAZEN BAREFACED LIE...
POP
POP
DIK BROWNE 2-4
HERE'S DADDY NOW...
HOW DID YOU DO WITH THE TAX MAN?
OKAY, I GUESS

The End

30 MILES TO A GALLON

HAW! GET A HORSE!
BEAT IT, YOU!!
WHAT DOES HE KNOW? IF YOU SAY YOU'RE A HORSE, THAT'S GOOD ENOUGH FOR ME!

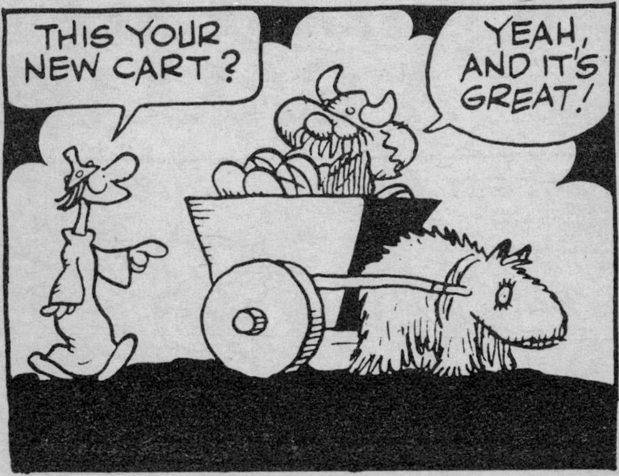
THIS YOUR NEW CART?
YEAH, AND IT'S GREAT!

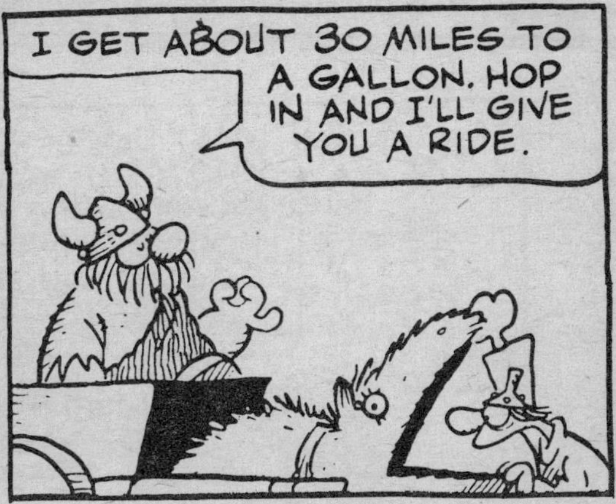
I GET ABOUT 30 MILES TO A GALLON. HOP IN AND I'LL GIVE YOU A RIDE.

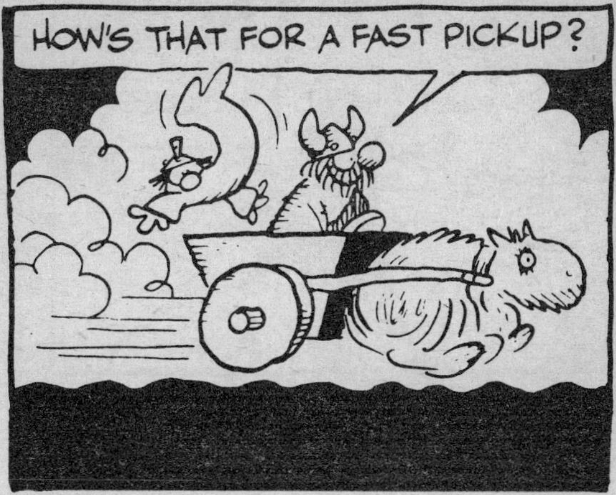
HOW'S THAT FOR A FAST PICKUP?

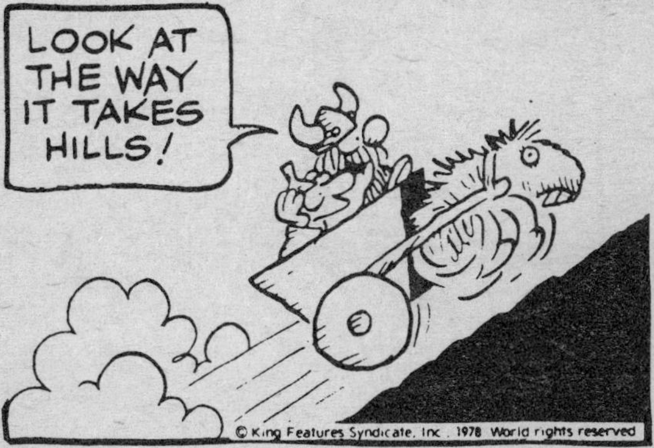
LOOK AT THE WAY IT TAKES HILLS!

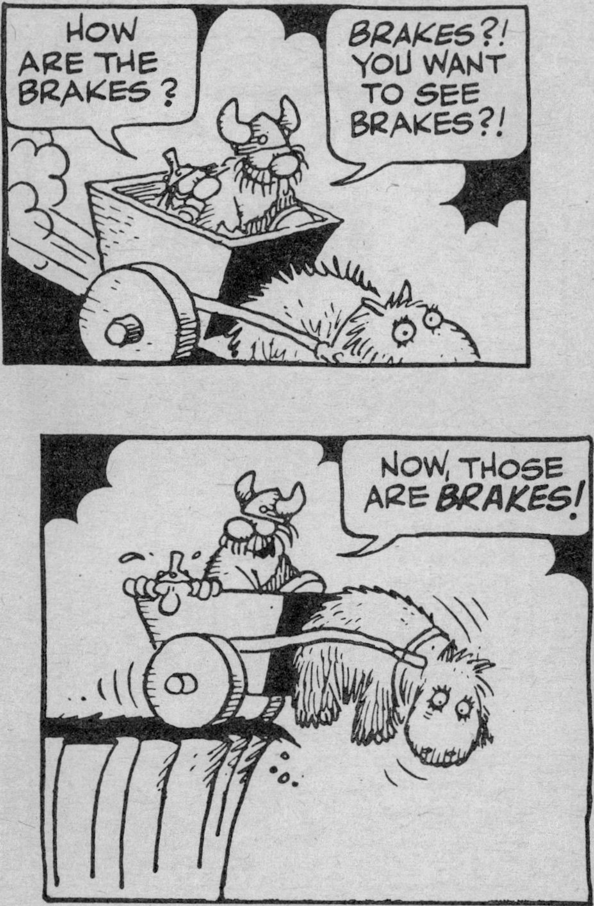
HOW ARE THE BRAKES ?
BRAKES?! YOU WANT TO SEE BRAKES?!
NOW, THOSE ARE BRAKES!

The End

FARE-WELL

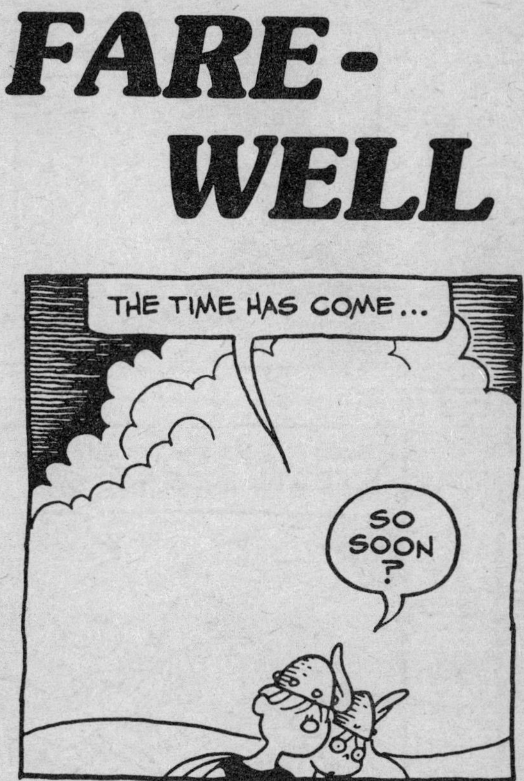
THE TIME HAS COME...
SO SOON ?

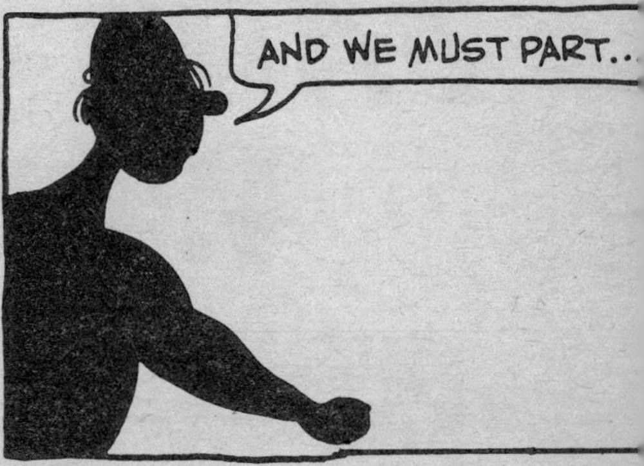
AND WE MUST PART...

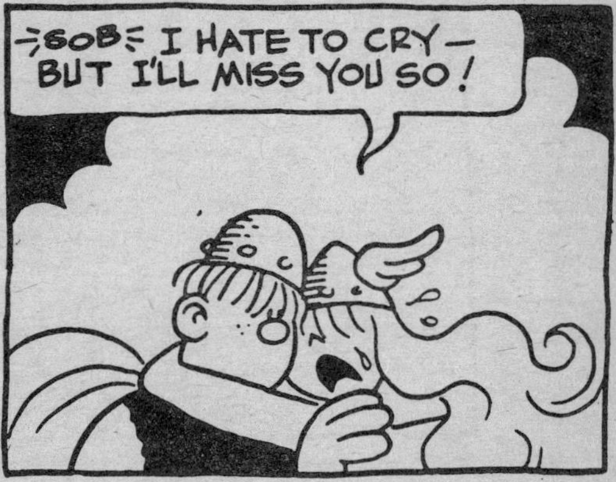
SOB I HATE TO CRY— BUT I'LL MISS YOU SO!

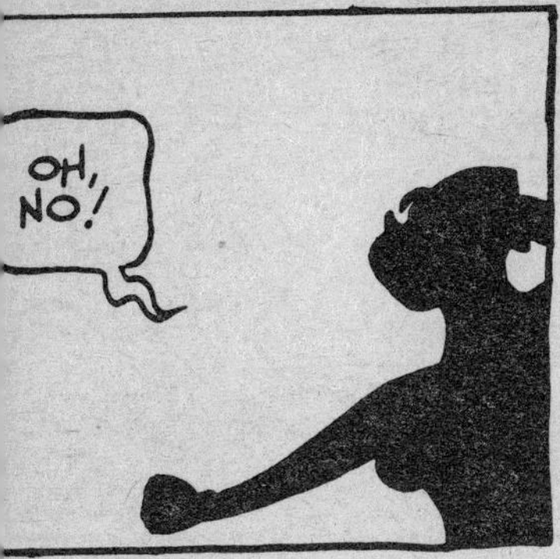
OH, NO!

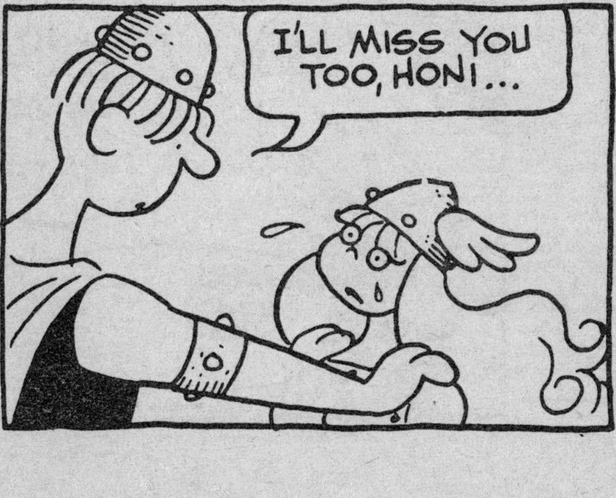
I'LL MISS YOU TOO, HONI...

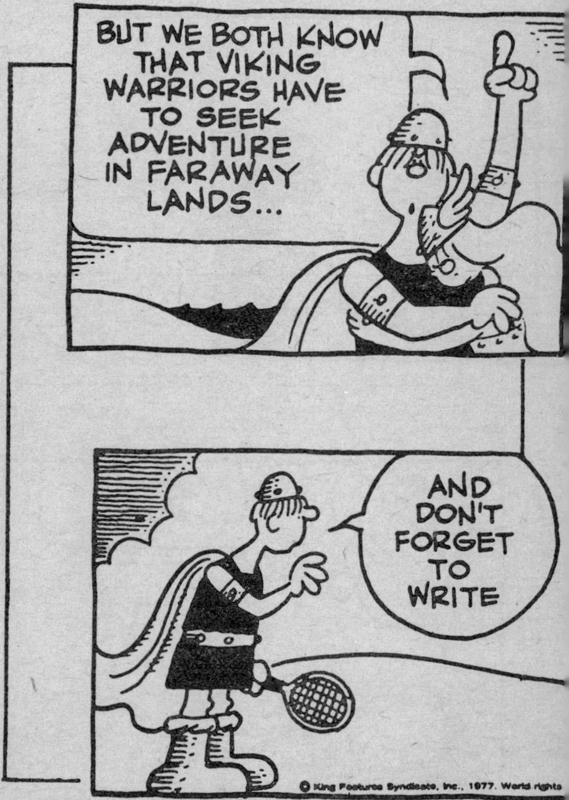
BUT WE BOTH KNOW THAT VIKING WARRIORS HAVE TO SEEK ADVENTURE IN FARAWAY LANDS...
AND DON'T FORGET TO WRITE
© King Features Syndicate, Inc., 1977. World rights

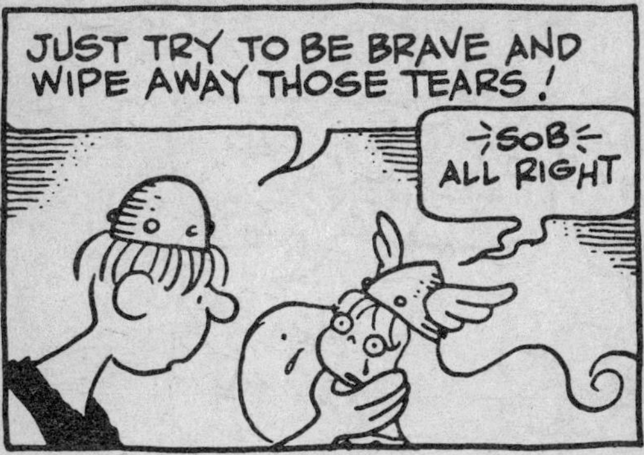
JUST TRY TO BE BRAVE AND WIPE AWAY THOSE TEARS!
SOB
ALL RIGHT

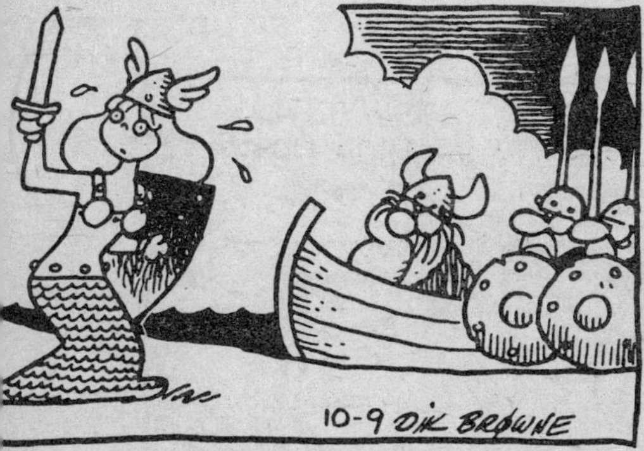
10-9 DIK BROWNE

The End

EDDIE'S

DUMB! DUMB! DUMB!
WHY IS HAGAR SO UPSET?
I JUST TOLD DAD THE WORLD WAS ROUND
WOW! THAT WOULD UPSET ANYBODY!

SPINNING

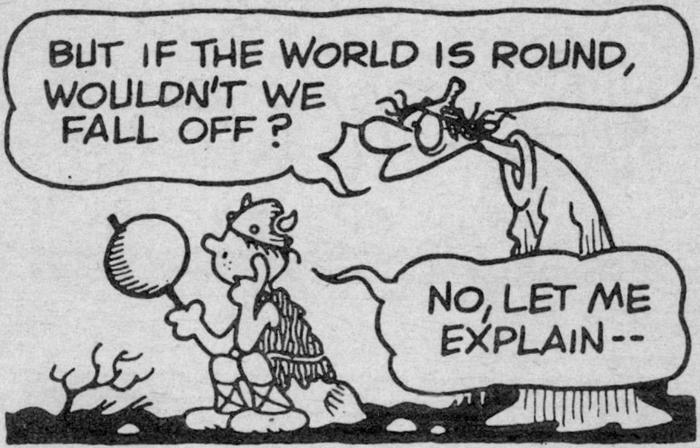
BUT IF THE WORLD IS ROUND, WOULDN'T WE FALL OFF ?
NO, LET ME EXPLAIN --

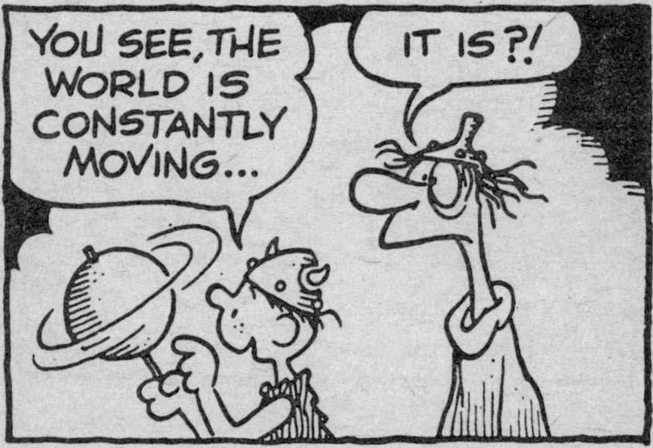
YOU SEE, THE WORLD IS CONSTANTLY MOVING...
IT IS?!

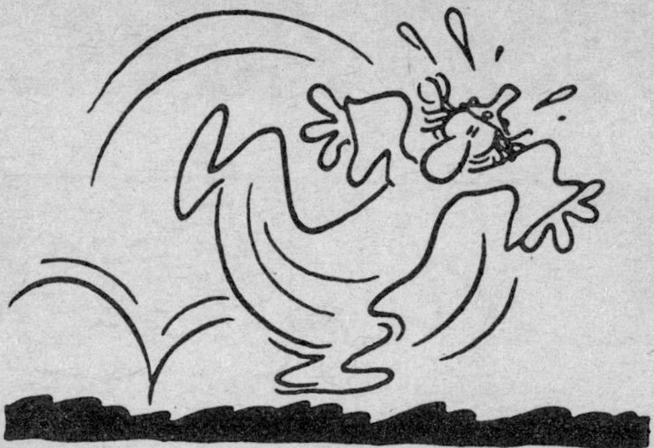

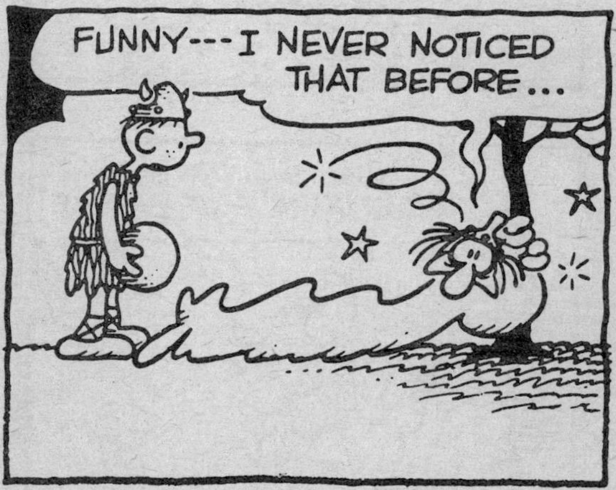
FUNNY---I NEVER NOTICED THAT BEFORE...

DISTANCE

TODAY-
THE TOOLS
OF THE
TRADE
THIS IS A JAVELIN-
THE PRINCE OF BATTLE!

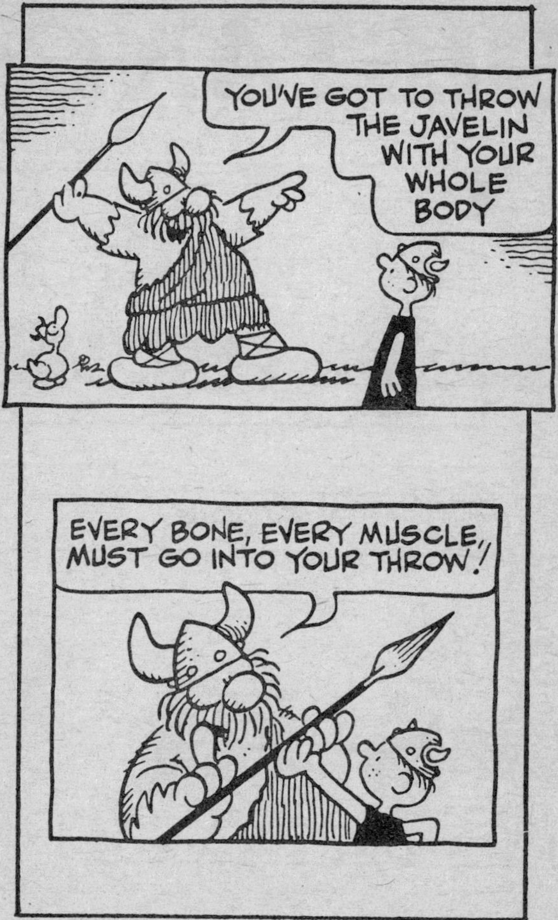
YOU'VE GOT TO THROW THE JAVELIN WITH YOUR WHOLE BODY
EVERY BONE, EVERY MUSCLE, MUST GO INTO YOUR THROW!

GRIT YOUR TEETH! YOU ARE ABOUT TO THROW A THUNDERBOLT!
NOW THROW!
© King Features Syndicate, Inc. 1978 World rights reserved

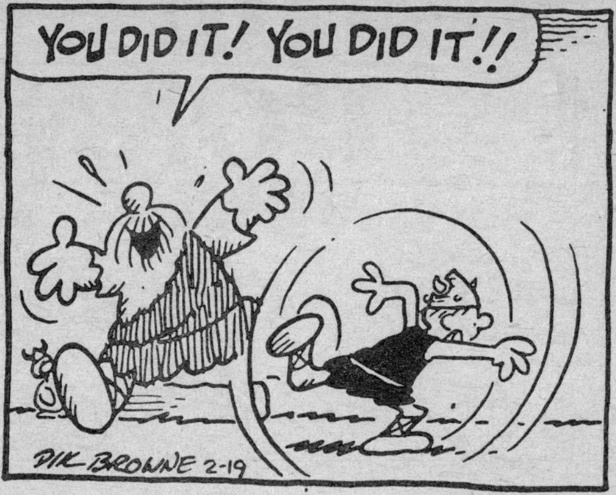
YOU DID IT! YOU DID IT!!
DIK BROWNE 2-19

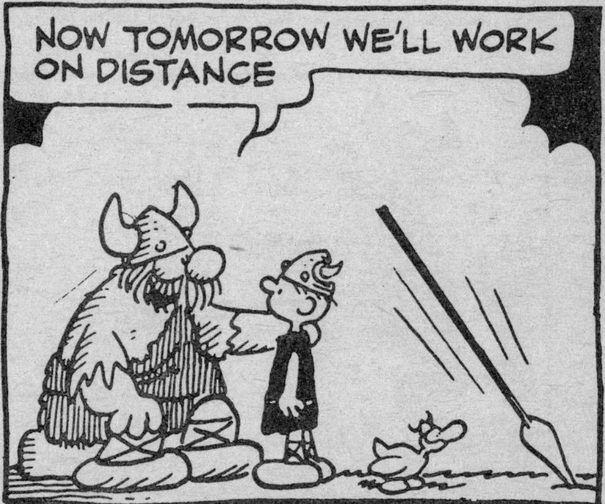
NOW TOMORROW WE'LL WORK ON DISTANCE

The End

8-9-10! BONK!

BOY! YOU KNOW YOUR WAY AROUND!
AND WHY NOT?!
WHEN I WAS A KID
I COULD SKIP A STON
10 TIMES ON THAT LAK
AND HIT THAT ROC

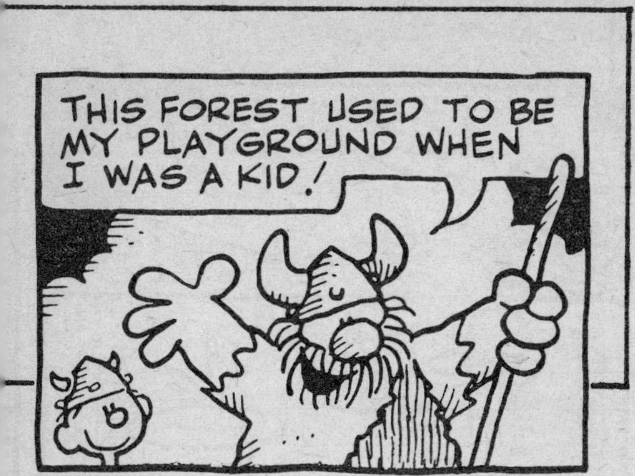
THIS FOREST USED TO BE MY PLAYGROUND WHEN I WAS A KID!

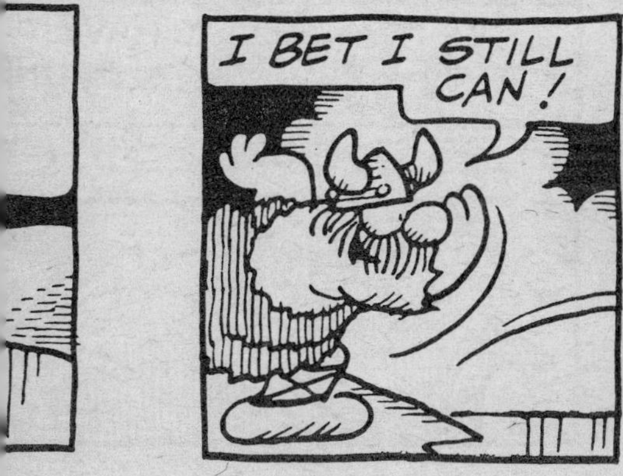
I BET I STILL CAN!

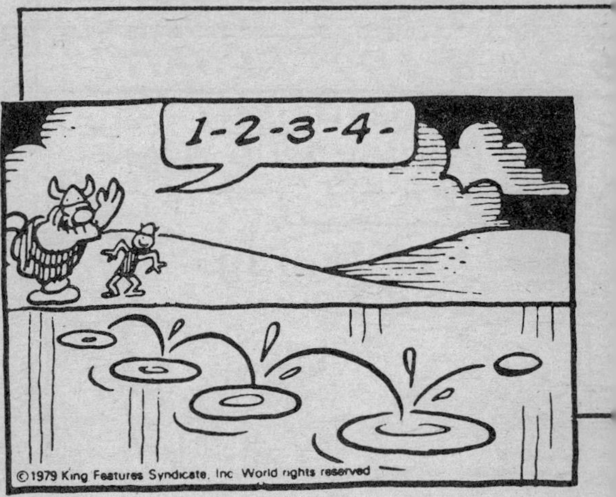
1-2-3-4-
©1979 King Features Syndicate, Inc World rights reserved

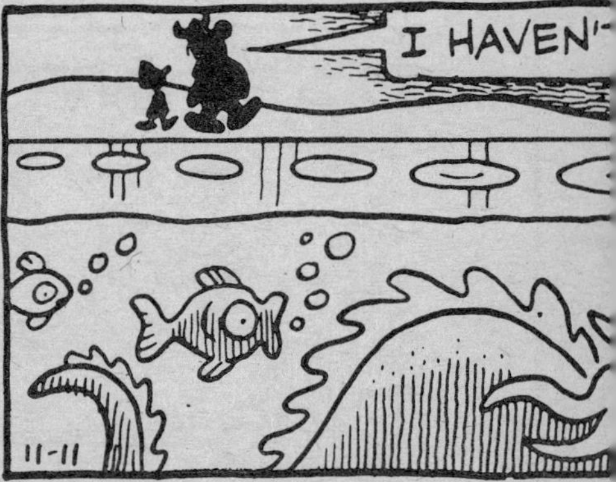
I HAVEN'
11-11

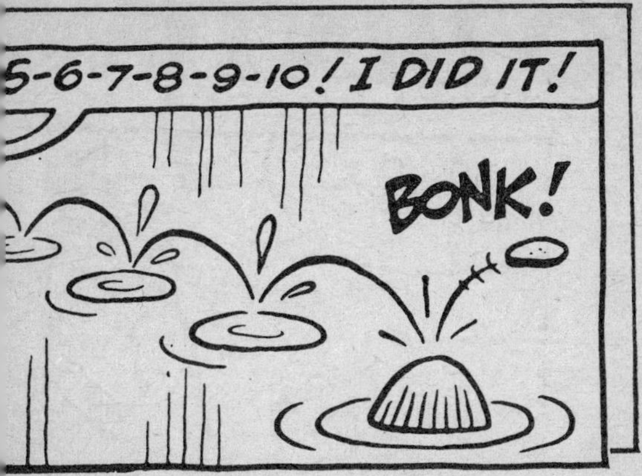

5-6-7-8-9-10! I DID IT!
BONK!

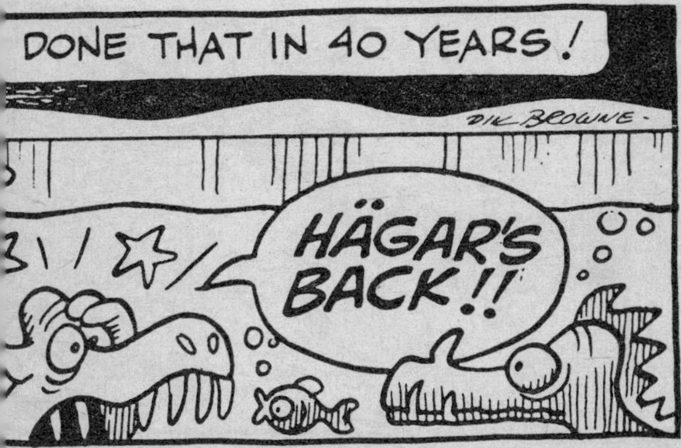

DONE THAT IN 40 YEARS!
DIK BROWNE
HÄGAR'S BACK!!

The End

NO HINTING

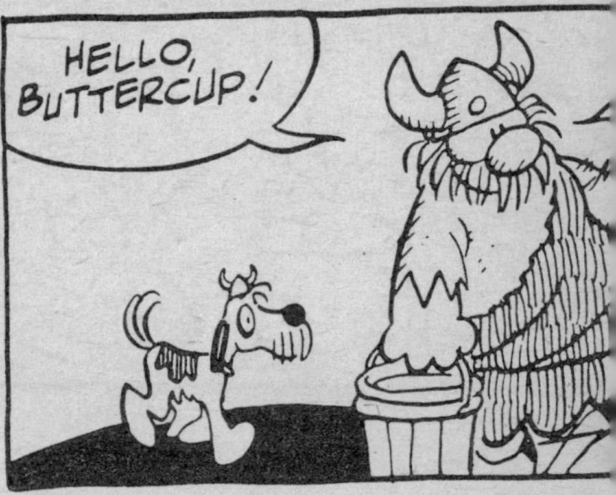
HELLO, BUTTERCUP!

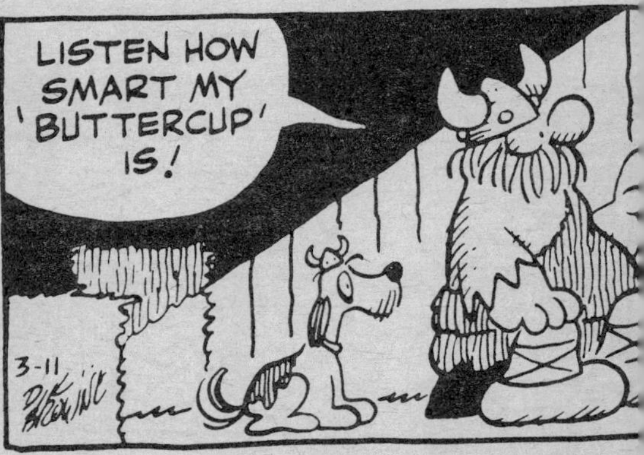
LISTEN HOW SMART MY 'BUTTERCUP' IS!
3-11

MAYBE YOU'RE NOT SO PRETTY BUT YOU'RE ONE SMART HORSE
COUNT TO FOUR!

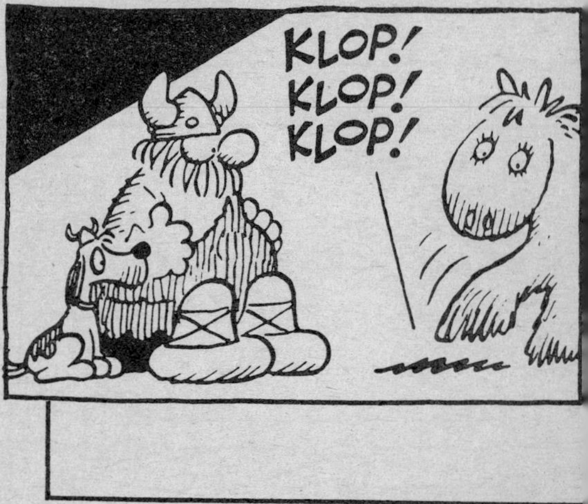
KLOP!
KLOP!
KLOP!

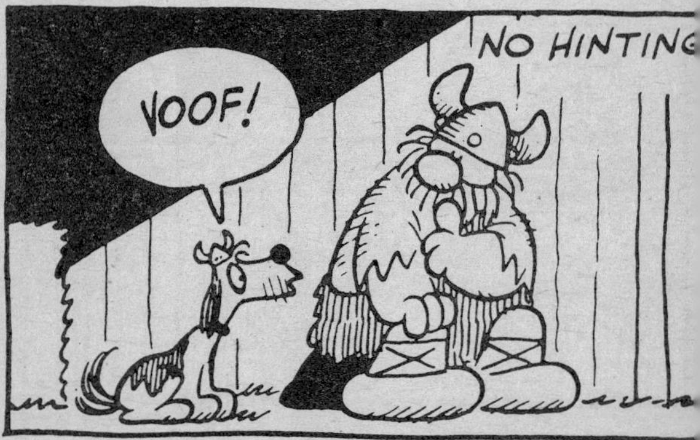
VOOF!
NO HINTING

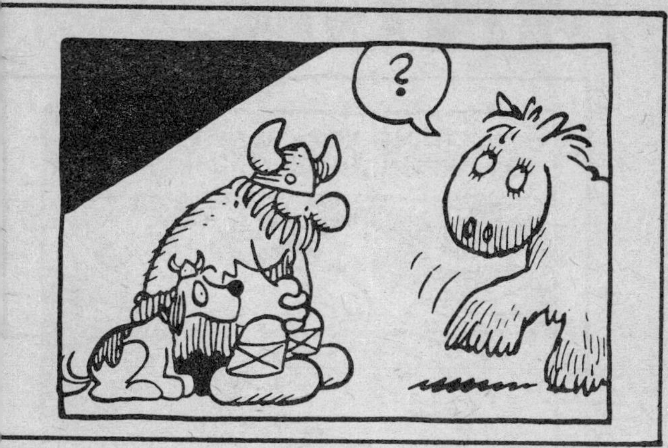
?

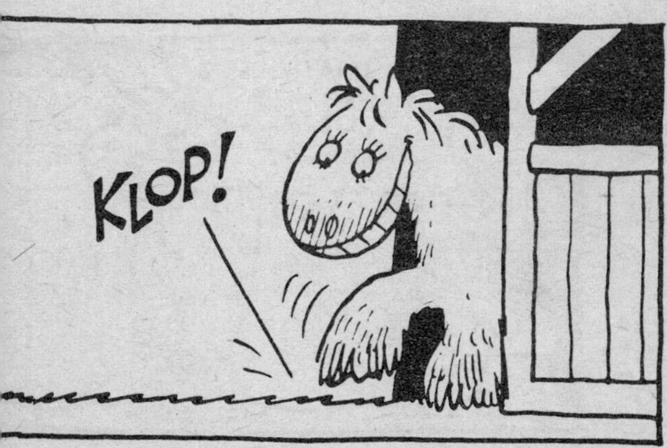
KLOP!

The End

MAGIC

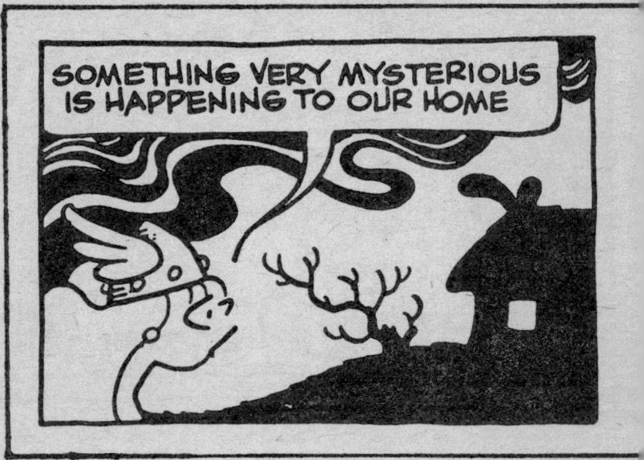
SOMETHING VERY MYSTERIOUS IS HAPPENING TO OUR HOME

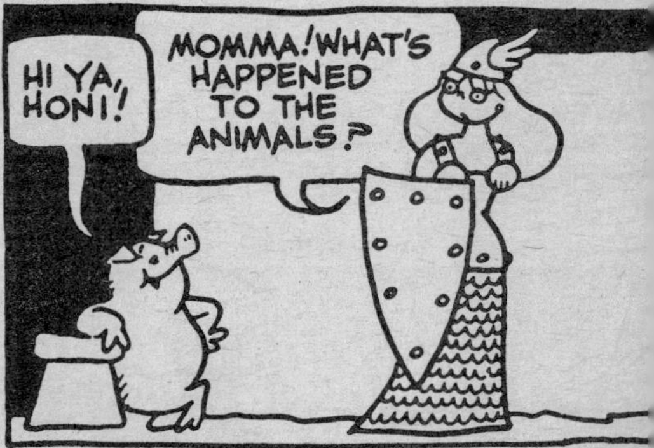
HI YA, HONI!
MOMMA! WHAT'S HAPPENED TO THE ANIMALS?

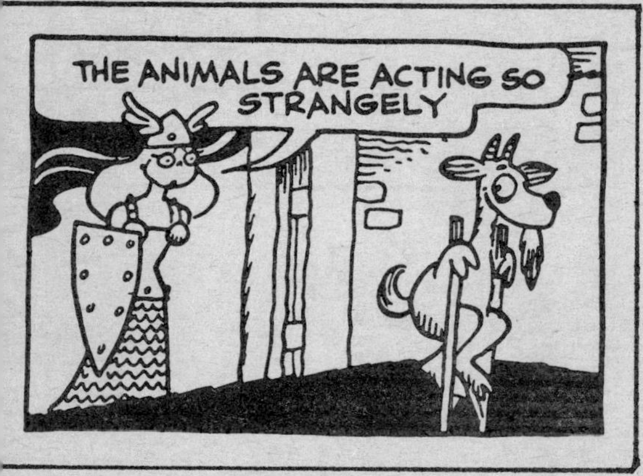
THE ANIMALS ARE ACTING SO STRANGELY

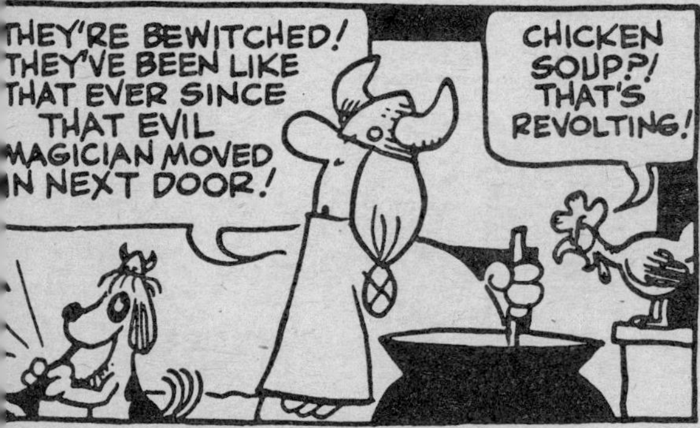
THEY'RE BEWITCHED! THEY'VE BEEN LIKE THAT EVER SINCE THAT EVIL MAGICIAN MOVED IN NEXT DOOR!
CHICKEN SOUP?! THAT'S REVOLTING!

WE CAN'T LET HIM GET AWAY WITH THIS!
OINK
WELL, WHAT DID HE SAY?!

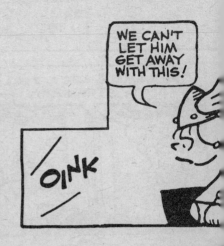

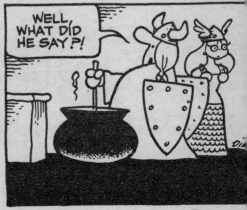

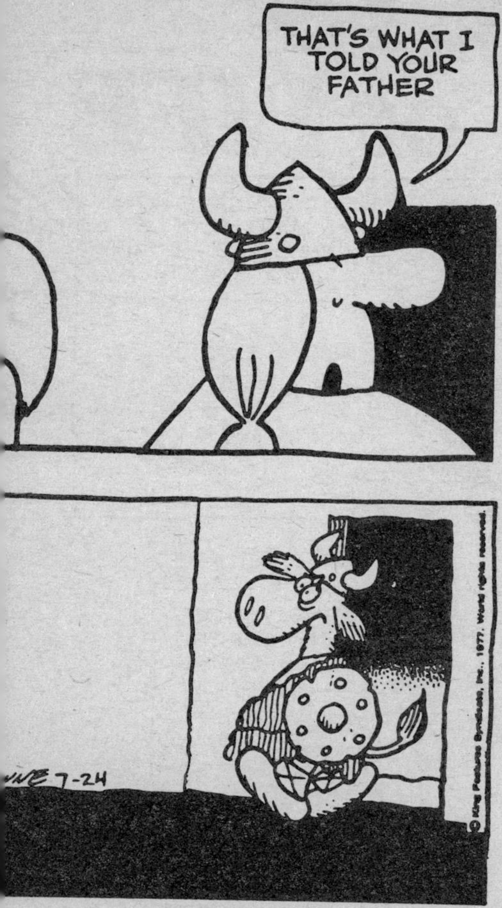
THAT'S WHAT I TOLD YOUR FATHER
© King Features Syndicate, Inc., 1977. World rights reserved.

The End

FACTS OF LIFE

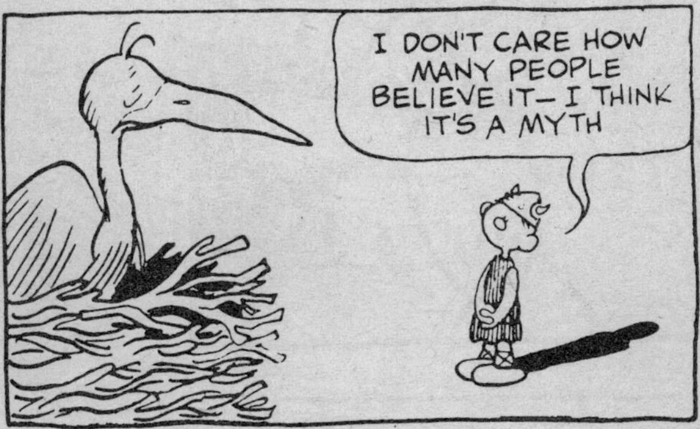
I DON'T CARE HOW MANY PEOPLE BELIEVE IT— I THINK IT'S A MYTH

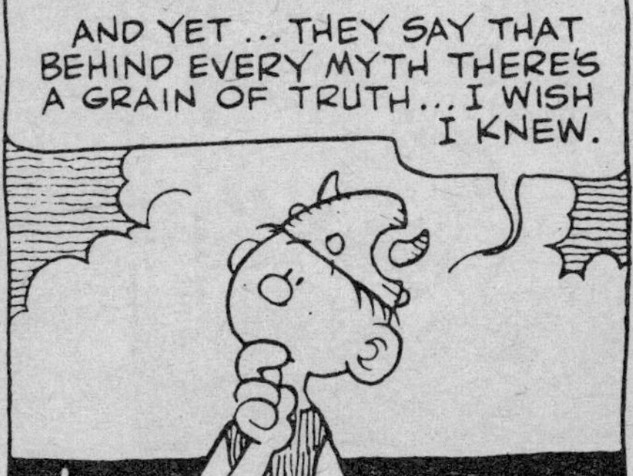
AND YET ... THEY SAY THAT BEHIND EVERY MYTH THERE'S A GRAIN OF TRUTH... I WISH I KNEW.

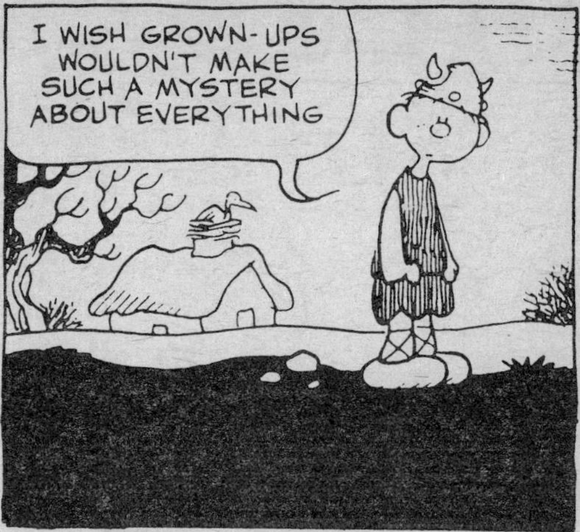
I WISH GROWN-UPS WOULDN'T MAKE SUCH A MYSTERY ABOUT EVERYTHING

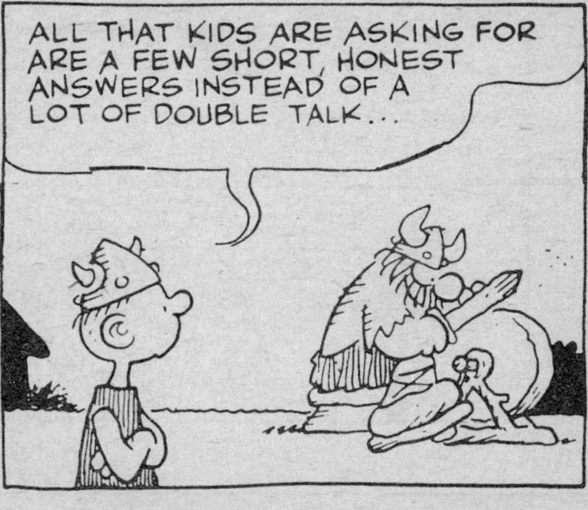
ALL THAT KIDS ARE ASKING FOR ARE A FEW SHORT, HONEST ANSWERS INSTEAD OF A LOT OF DOUBLE TALK...

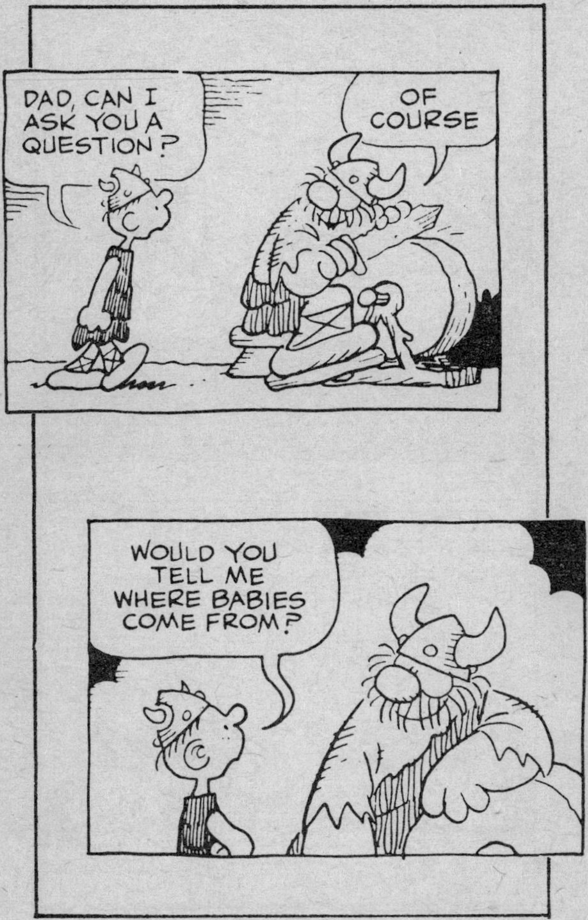
DAD, CAN I ASK YOU A QUESTION?
OF COURSE
WOULD YOU TELL ME WHERE BABIES COME FROM?

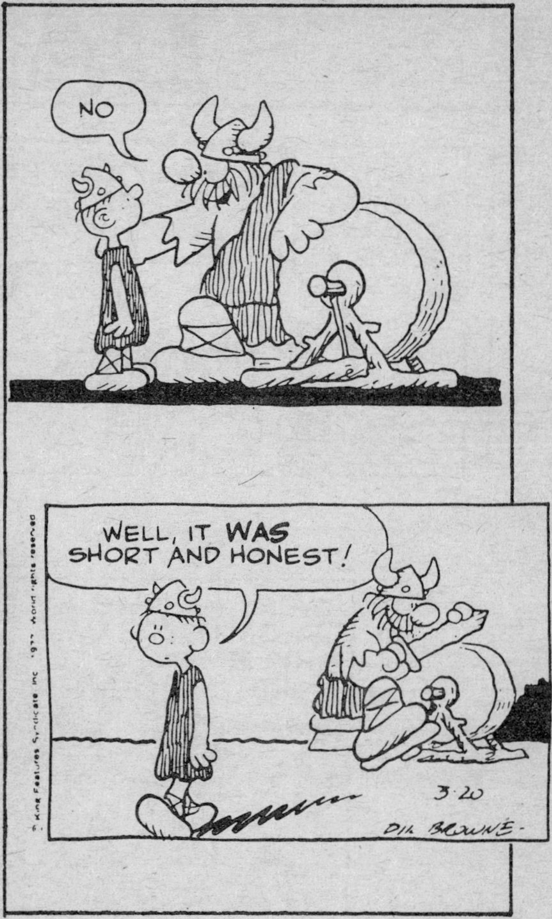
NO
WELL, IT WAS SHORT AND HONEST!
3·20
DIK BROWNE
© King Features Syndicate Inc
World rights reserved

The End

DAY

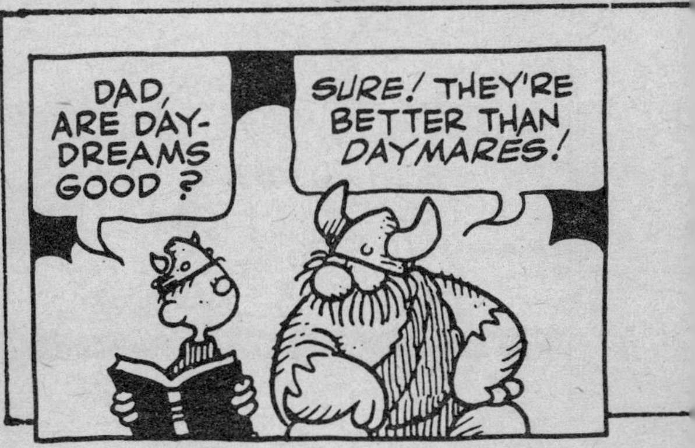

DAD, ARE DAY-DREAMS GOOD ?
SURE! THEY'RE BETTER THAN DAYMARES!

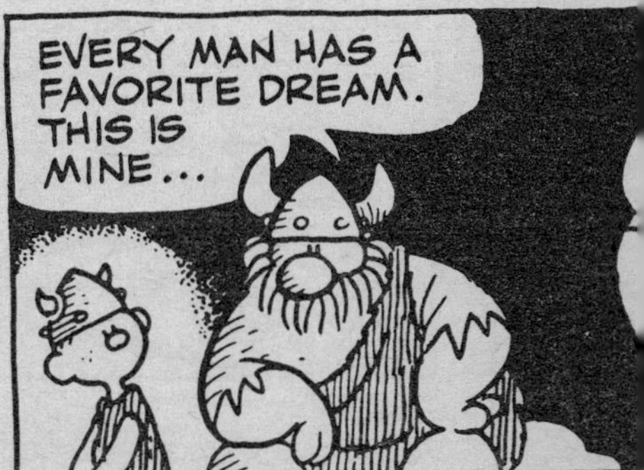

EVERY MAN HAS A FAVORITE DREAM. THIS IS MINE...

DREAMS

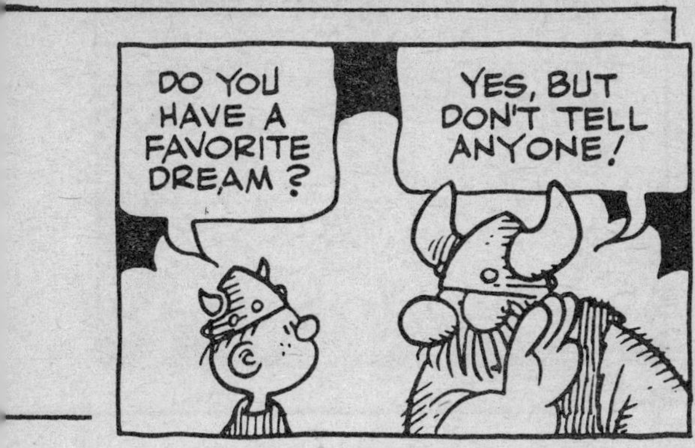
DO YOU HAVE A FAVORITE DREAM?
YES, BUT DON'T TELL ANYONE!

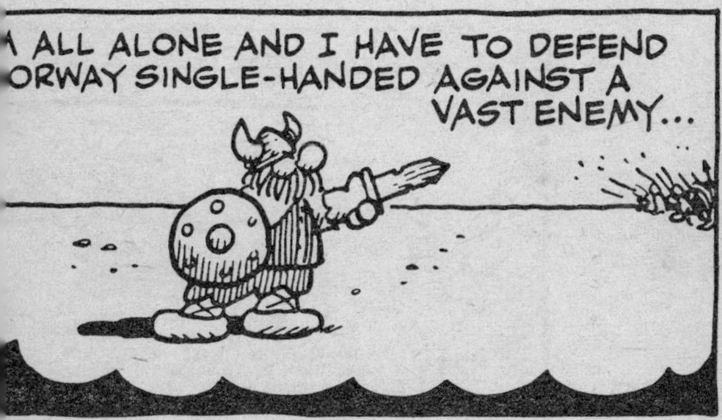
ALL ALONE AND I HAVE TO DEFEND
ORWAY SINGLE-HANDED AGAINST A VAST ENEMY...

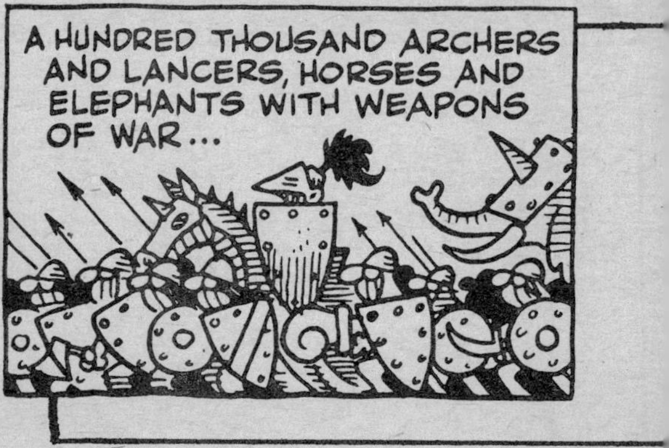
A HUNDRED THOUSAND ARCHERS AND LANCERS, HORSES AND ELEPHANTS WITH WEAPONS OF WAR...

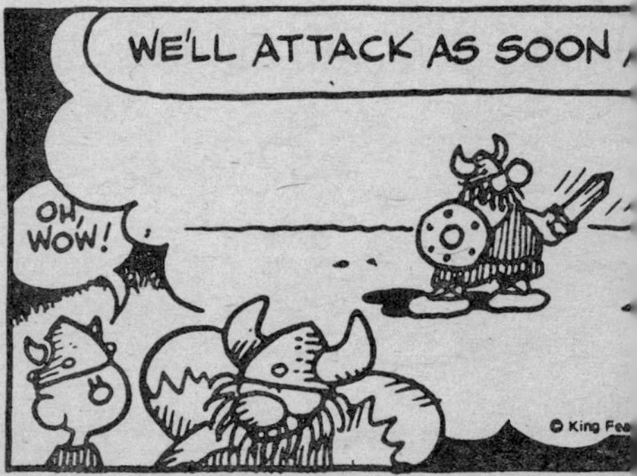
WE'LL ATTACK AS SOON
OH, WOW!

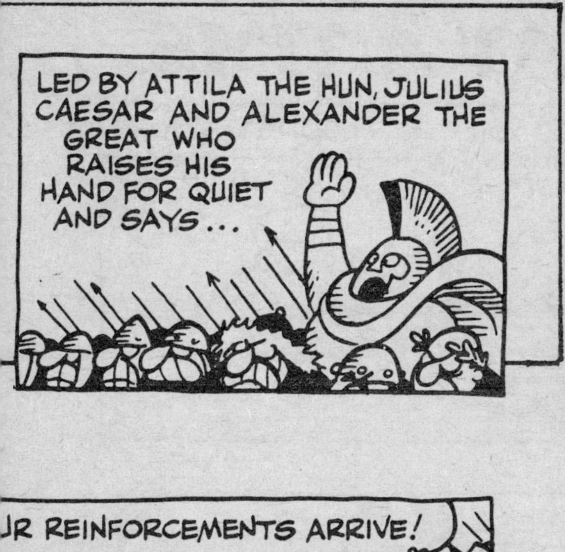
LED BY ATTILA THE HUN, JULIUS CAESAR AND ALEXANDER THE GREAT WHO RAISES HIS HAND FOR QUIET AND SAYS...

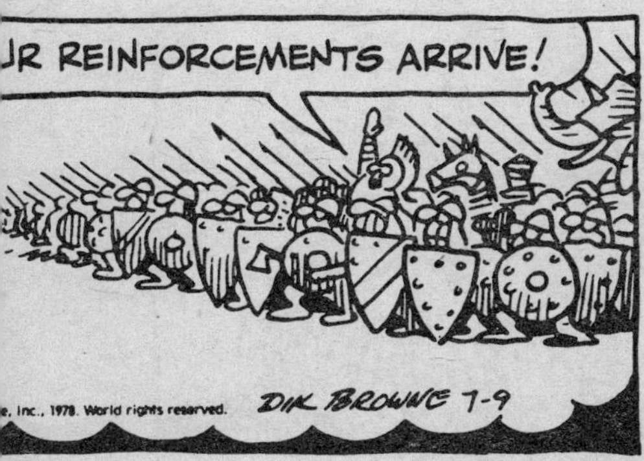
JR REINFORCEMENTS ARRIVE!
e, Inc., 1978. World rights reserved.
DIK BROWNE 7-9

The End

ONE THING AT A TIME

ARE YOU THINKING, DADDY ?
NO, MY SON, I'M SITTING
WHEN I SIT I SIT AND WHEN I THINK I THINK!

REMEMBER, MY SON— "NEVER CHASE TWO RABBITS"
LET ME EXPLAIN...
WOOSH!
© King Features Syndicate, Inc., 1978. World rights reserved.

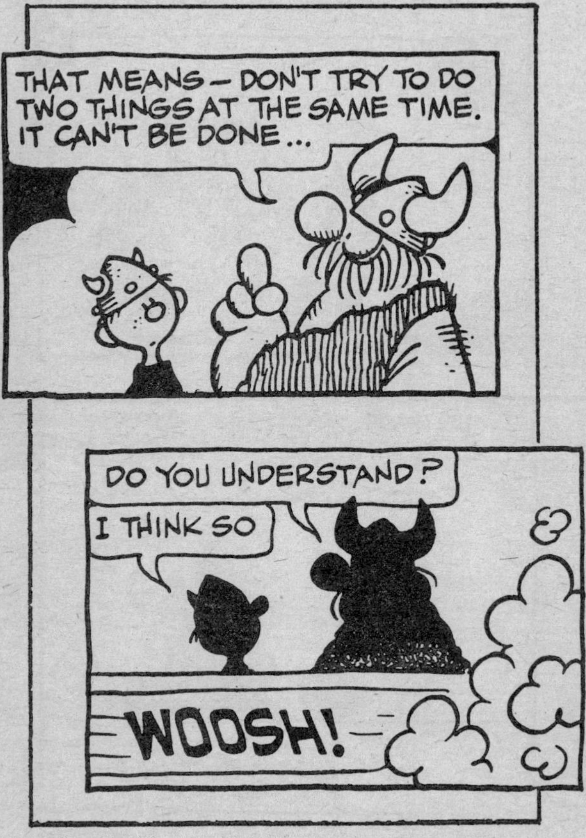
THAT MEANS — DON'T TRY TO DO TWO THINGS AT THE SAME TIME. IT CAN'T BE DONE...
DO YOU UNDERSTAND?
I THINK SO
WOOSH!

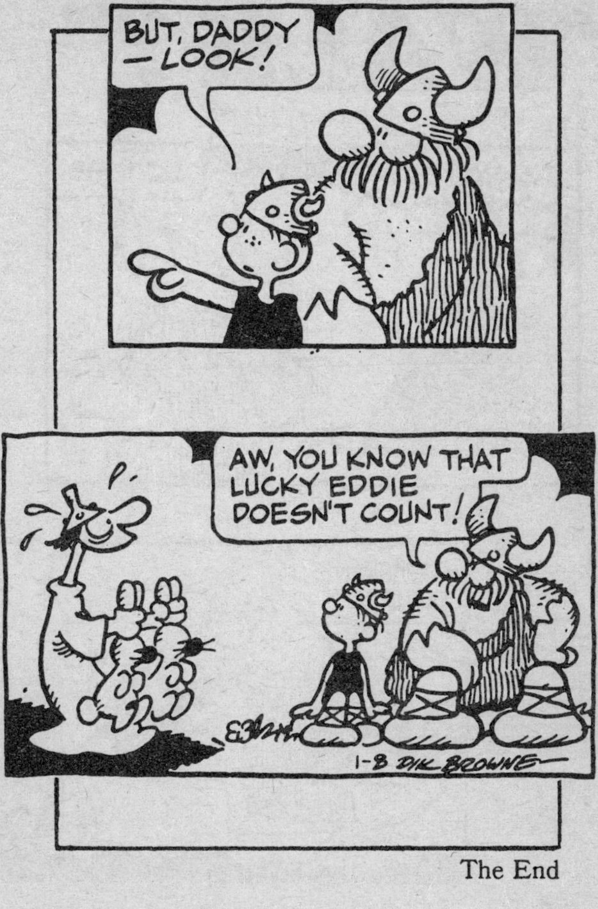
BUT, DADDY
—LOOK!
AW, YOU KNOW THAT
LUCKY EDDIE
DOESN'T COUNT!
1-8 DIK BROWNE

The End

"WALK?"

DID YOU SAY SOMETHING?
NOT ME
SOMEONE DID...
VOOF!

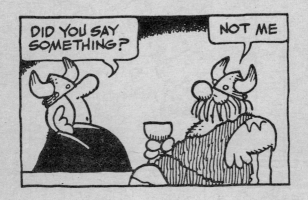

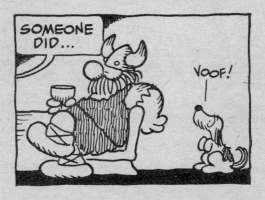

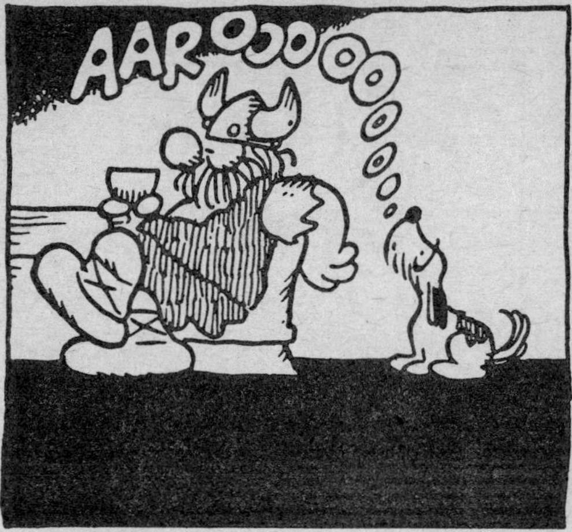
AAROOOOOOOOOO

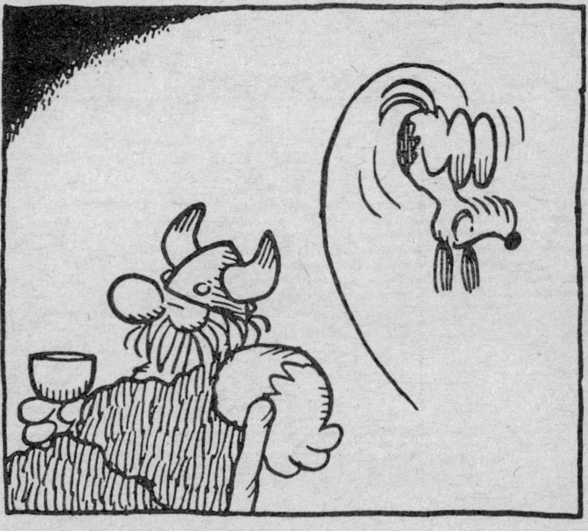

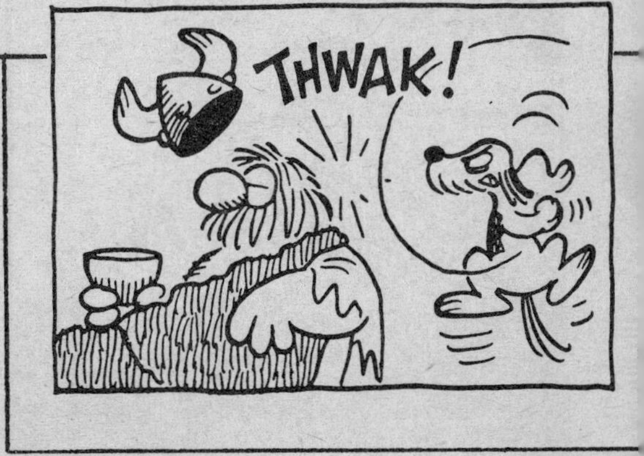
THWAK!

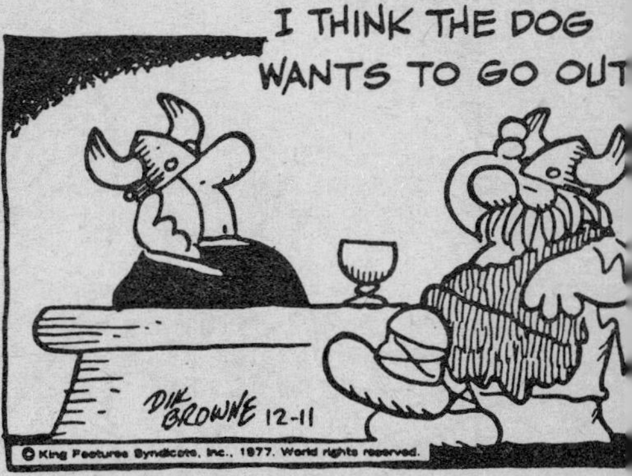
I THINK THE DOG
WANTS TO GO OUT
DIK BROWNE 12-11
© King Features Syndicate, Inc., 1977. World rights reserved.

CHOMP!

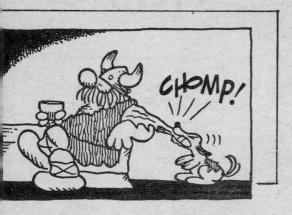

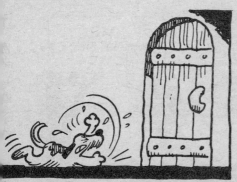

The End

THREE WISHES

I WONDER WHAT MAMA'S YELLING ABOUT?
STUPID!
DUMB!
UGH!
OH... DADDY MUST BE HOME...

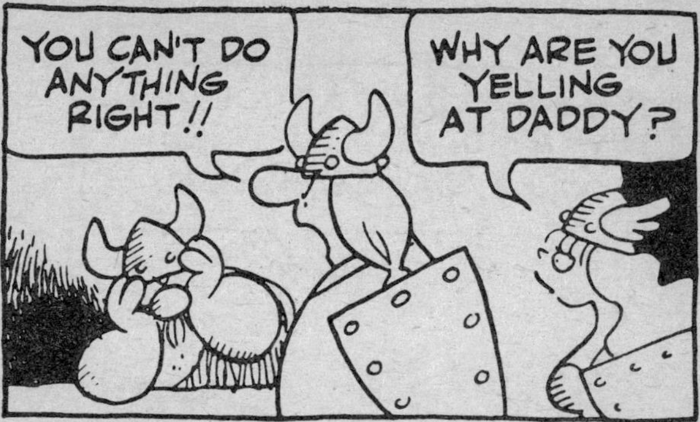
YOU CAN'T DO ANYTHING RIGHT!!
WHY ARE YOU YELLING AT DADDY?

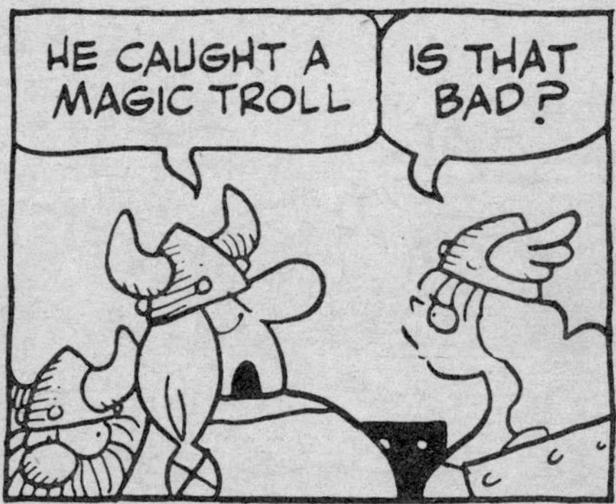
HE CAUGHT A MAGIC TROLL
IS THAT BAD?

NO! IT'S GREAT! A TROLL WILL GIVE ANYTHING TO BE FREED! MONEY! JEWELS! POWER!

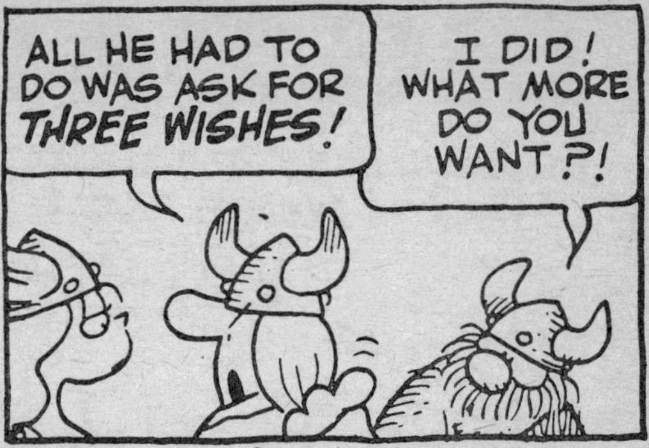
ALL HE HAD TO DO WAS ASK FOR THREE WISHES!
I DID! WHAT MORE DO YOU WANT ?!

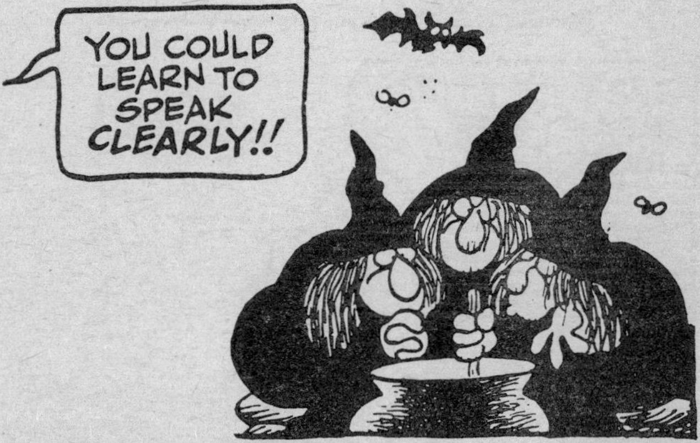
YOU COULD LEARN TO SPEAK CLEARLY!!

DIK BROWNE

The End

BIG DATE

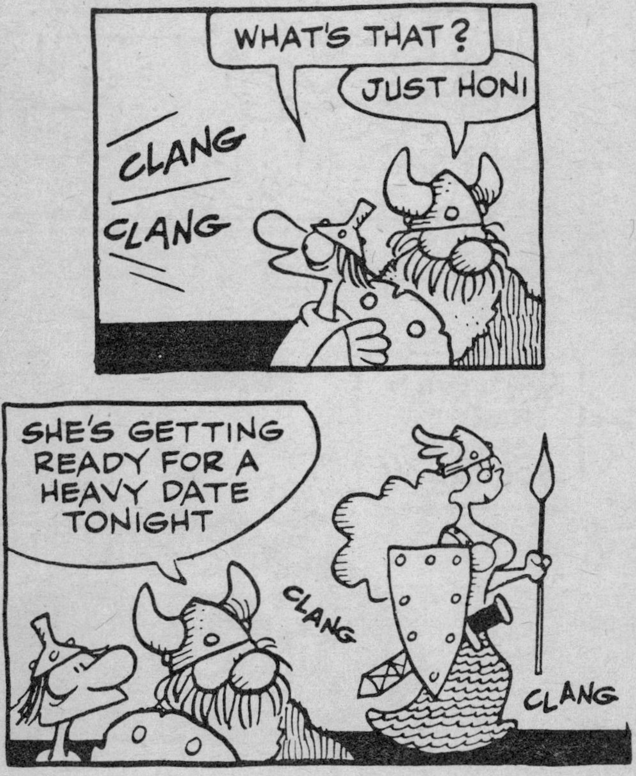
WHAT'S THAT?
JUST HONI
CLANG
CLANG
SHE'S GETTING READY FOR A HEAVY DATE TONIGHT
CLANG
CLANG

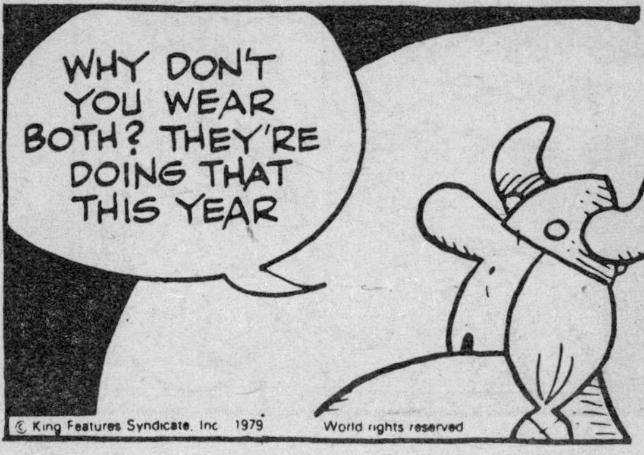
WHY DON'T YOU WEAR BOTH? THEY'RE DOING THAT THIS YEAR
© King Features Syndicate, Inc. 1979 World rights reserved

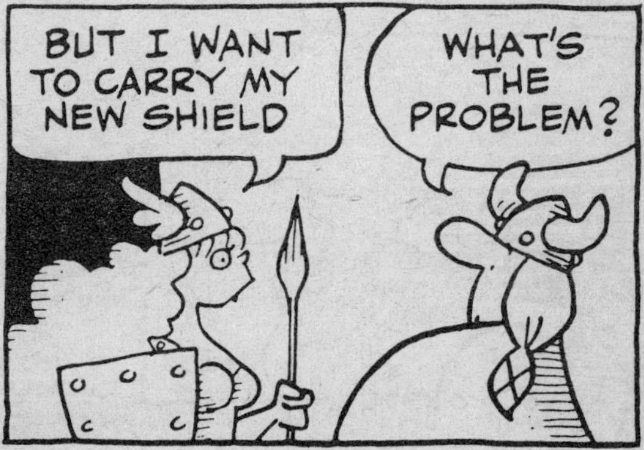
WHAT'S THE PROBLEM?
BUT I WANT TO CARRY MY NEW SHIELD

IT DOESN'T GO WITH MY SWORD
IT DOES CLASH A BIT
NOT TO WORRY, LUCKY EDDIE
I THINK I'LL JUST TAKE THE SPEAR
THAT'S SMART
2-25
DIK BROWNE

The End

FOR LOVE OR $

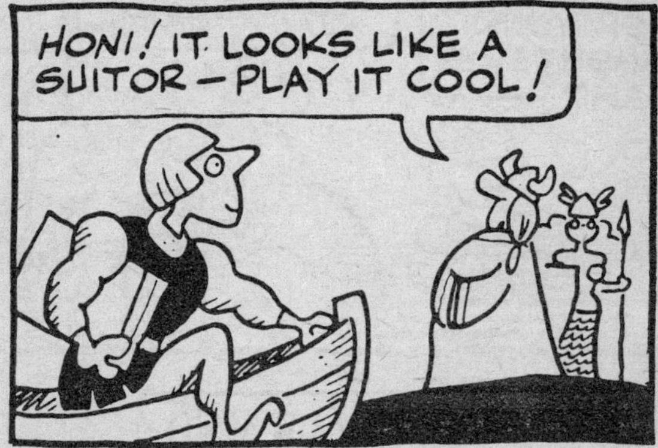
HONI! IT LOOKS LIKE A SUITOR—PLAY IT COOL!

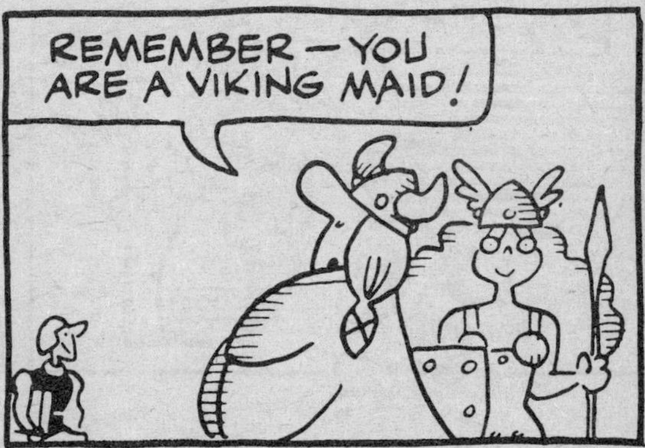
REMEMBER—YOU ARE A VIKING MAID!

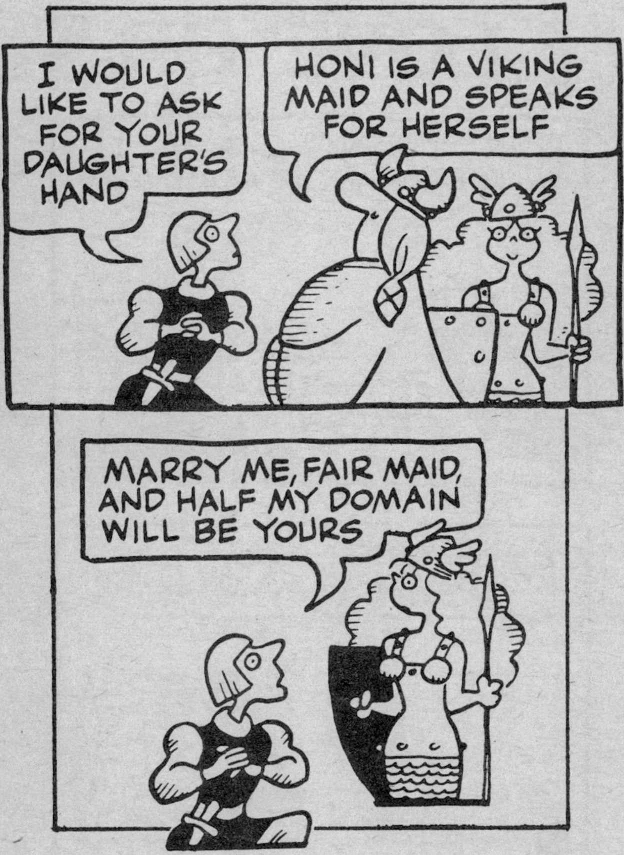
I WOULD LIKE TO ASK FOR YOUR DAUGHTER'S HAND
HONI IS A VIKING MAID AND SPEAKS FOR HERSELF
MARRY ME, FAIR MAID, AND HALF MY DOMAIN WILL BE YOURS

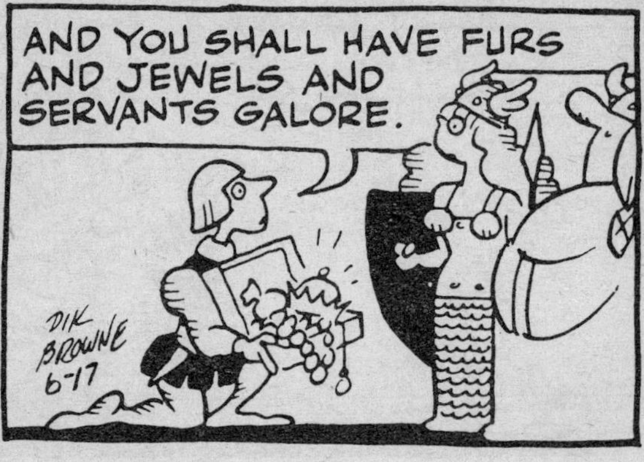
AND YOU SHALL HAVE FURS AND JEWELS AND SERVANTS GALORE.
DIK BROWNE 6-17

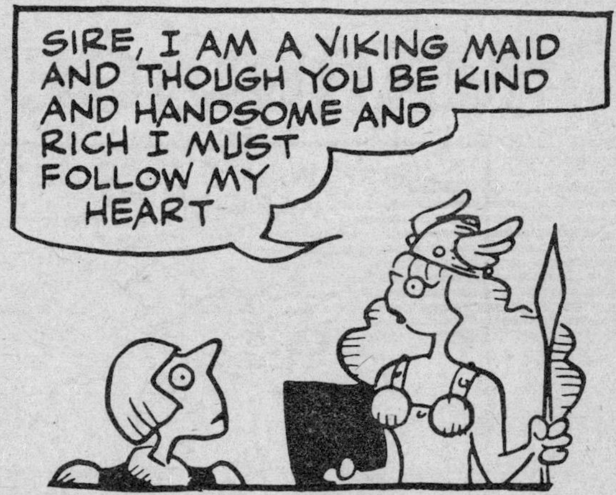
SIRE, I AM A VIKING MAID AND THOUGH YOU BE KIND AND HANDSOME AND RICH I MUST FOLLOW MY HEART

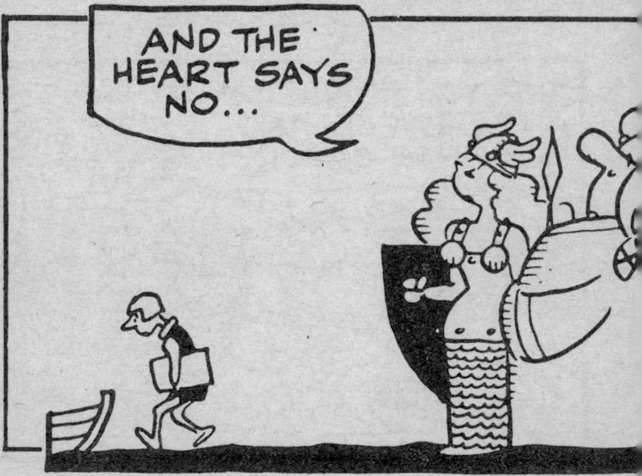
AND THE HEART SAYS NO...

MARRIAGE

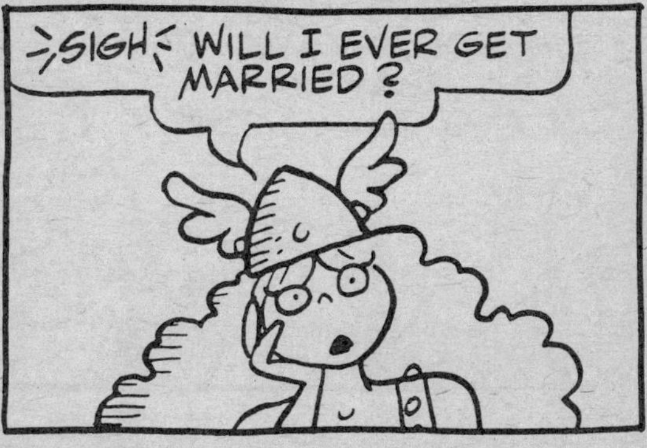
SIGH WILL I EVER GET MARRIED?

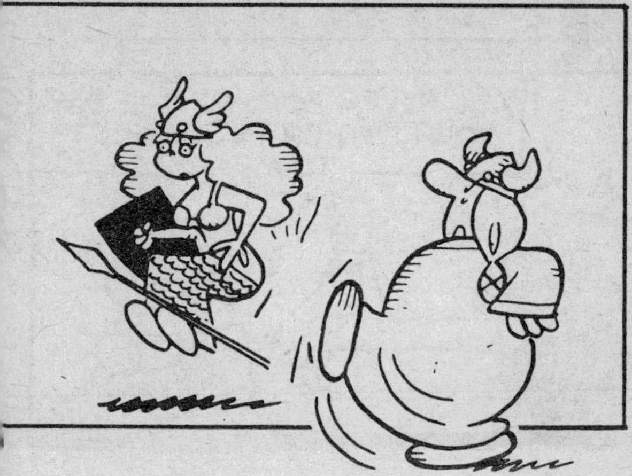

The End

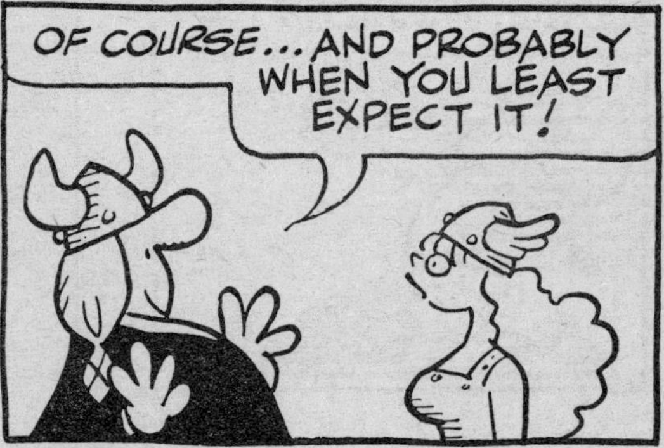
OF COURSE...AND PROBABLY WHEN YOU LEAST EXPECT IT!

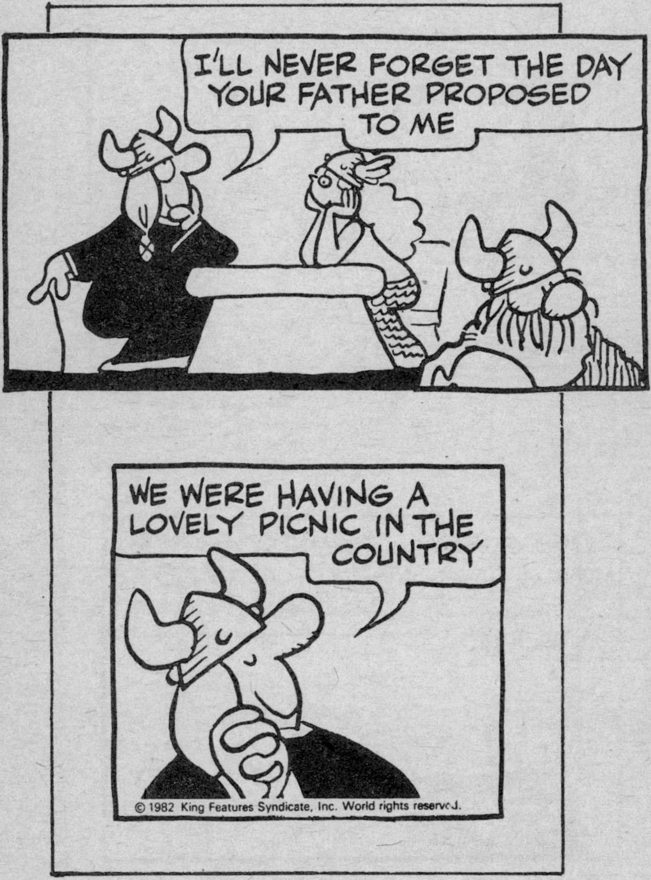
I'LL NEVER FORGET THE DAY YOUR FATHER PROPOSED TO ME
WE WERE HAVING A LOVELY PICNIC IN THE COUNTRY

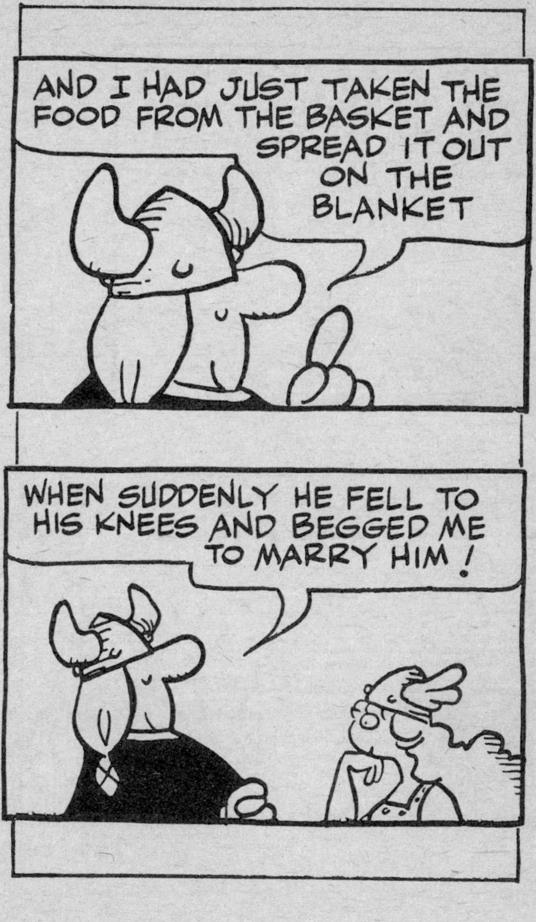
AND I HAD JUST TAKEN THE FOOD FROM THE BASKET AND SPREAD IT OUT ON THE BLANKET
WHEN SUDDENLY HE FELL TO HIS KNEES AND BEGGED ME TO MARRY HIM !

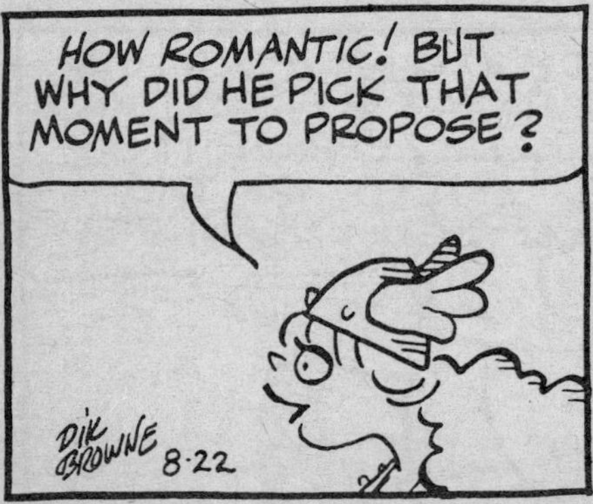
HOW ROMANTIC! BUT WHY DID HE PICK THAT MOMENT TO PROPOSE?
DIK BROWNE 8·22

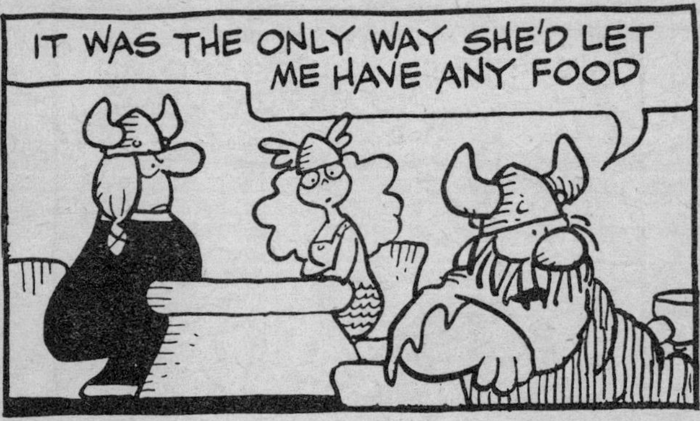
IT WAS THE ONLY WAY SHE'D LET ME HAVE ANY FOOD

The End

PIGEONS

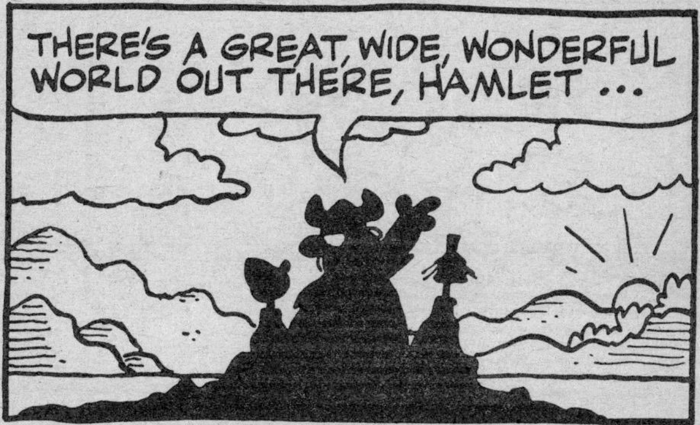
THERE'S A GREAT, WIDE, WONDERFUL WORLD OUT THERE, HAMLET ...

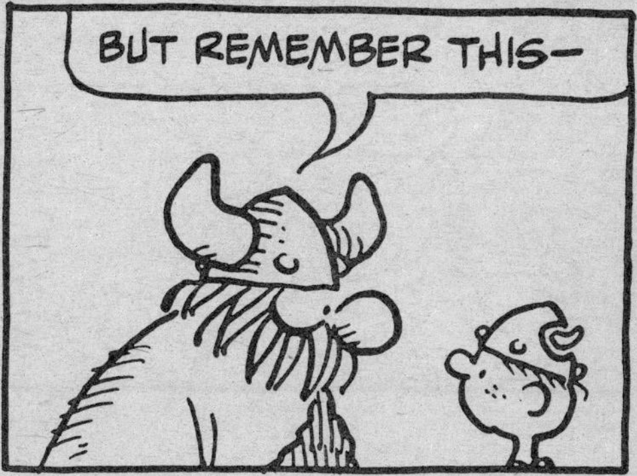
BUT REMEMBER THIS—

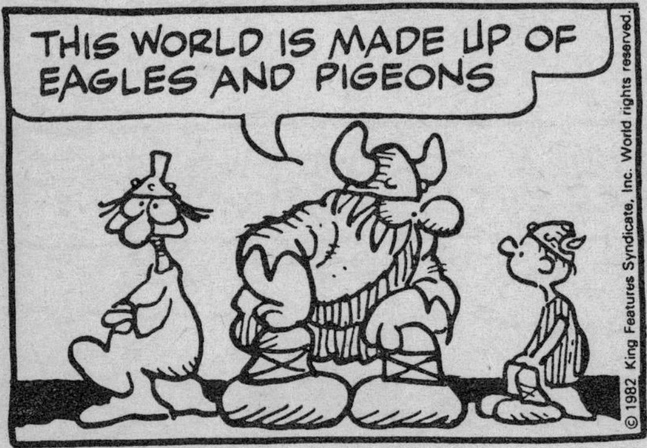
THIS WORLD IS MADE UP OF EAGLES AND PIGEONS
© 1982 King Features Syndicate, Inc. World rights reserved.

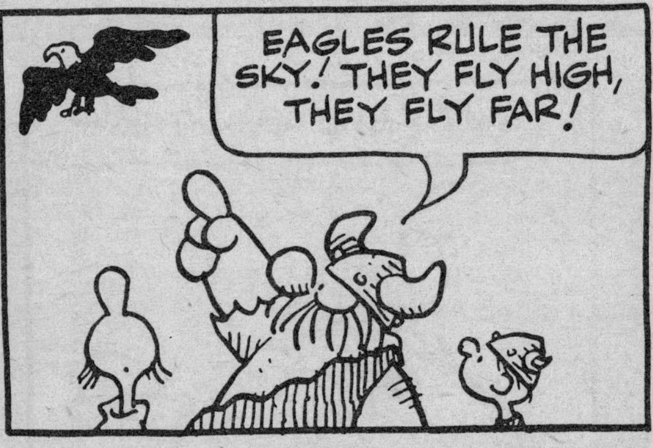
EAGLES RULE THE SKY! THEY FLY HIGH, THEY FLY FAR!

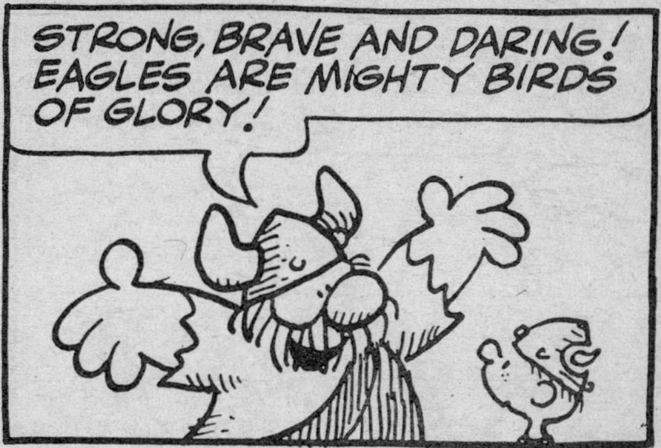
STRONG, BRAVE AND DARING! EAGLES ARE MIGHTY BIRDS OF GLORY!

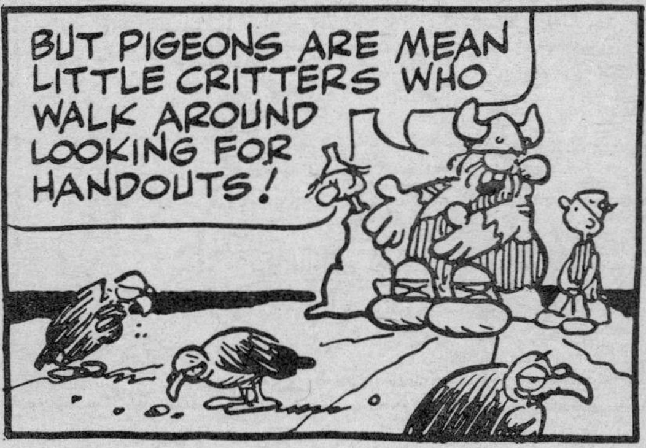
BUT PIGEONS ARE MEAN LITTLE CRITTERS WHO WALK AROUND LOOKING FOR HANDOUTS!

IT'S THE SAME WITH PEOPLE—
THEY'RE EITHER EAGLES
OR PIGEONS!
WOW!
WHICH ARE WE?
DIK BROWNE
8-29

The End

NEVER KNEW

AREN'T YOU GOING TO TELL DADDY ABOUT THE PARTY ?
NOT NOW
I'LL TELL HIM WHEN HE'S NOT SO BUSY

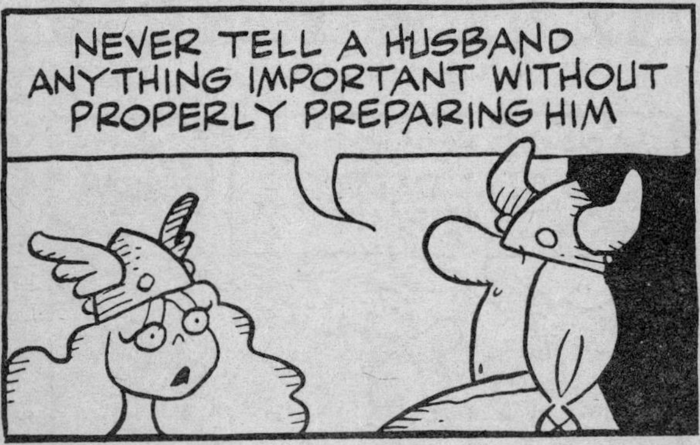
NEVER TELL A HUSBAND ANYTHING IMPORTANT WITHOUT PROPERLY PREPARING HIM

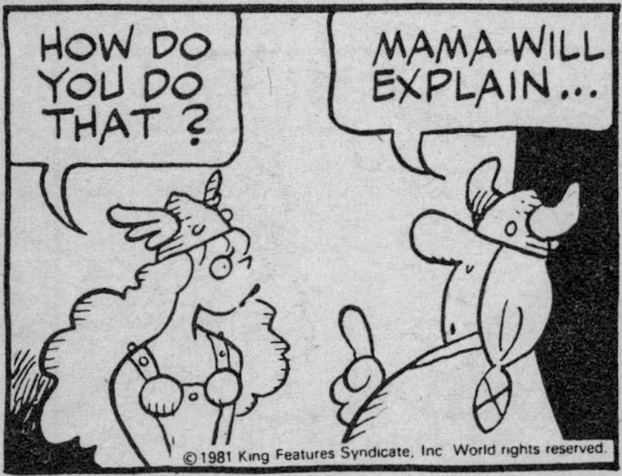
HOW DO YOU DO THAT ?
MAMA WILL EXPLAIN...
© 1981 King Features Syndicate, Inc. World rights reserved.

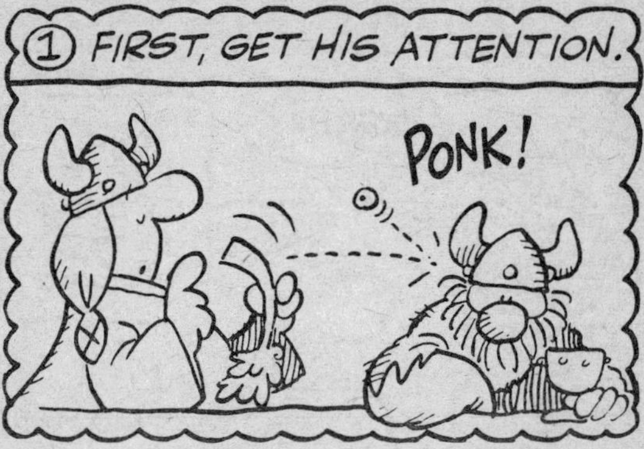
① FIRST, GET HIS ATTENTION.
PONK!

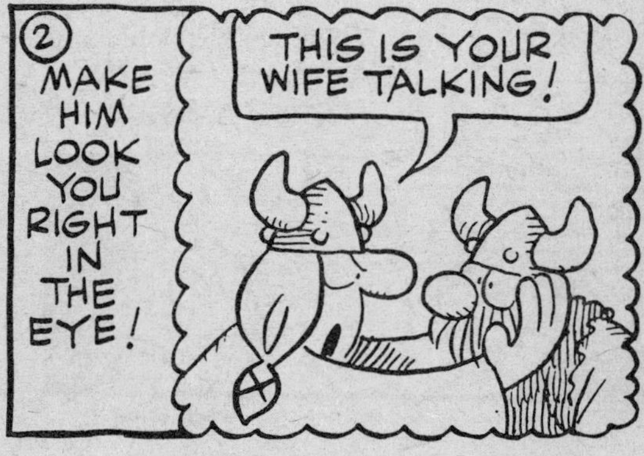
② MAKE HIM LOOK YOU RIGHT IN THE EYE!
THIS IS YOUR WIFE TALKING!

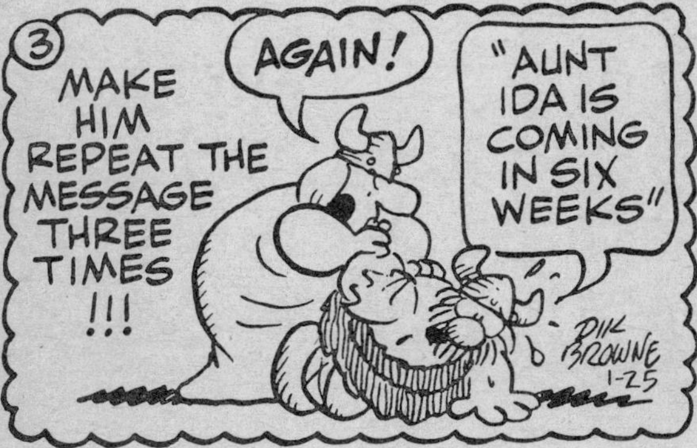
3
MAKE HIM REPEAT THE MESSAGE THREE TIMES !!!
AGAIN!
"AUNT IDA IS COMING IN SIX WEEKS"
DIK BROWNE 1-25

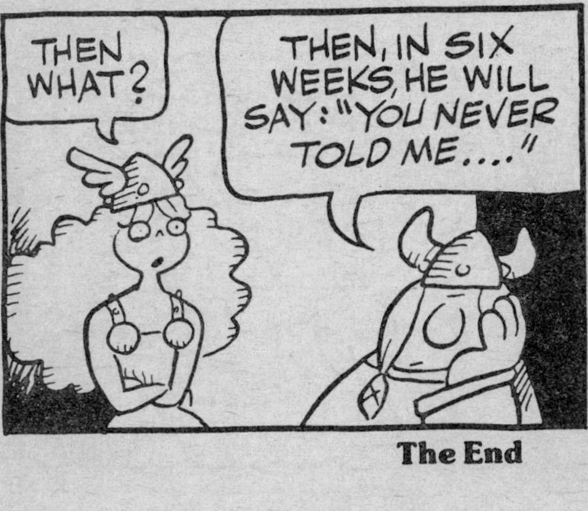
THEN WHAT?
THEN, IN SIX WEEKS, HE WILL SAY: "YOU NEVER TOLD ME...."

The End

IN-LAWS

DO WE HAVE TO GO TO ANOTHER REUNION ?
I DON'T CARE...
THEY'RE YOUR RELATIVES
?

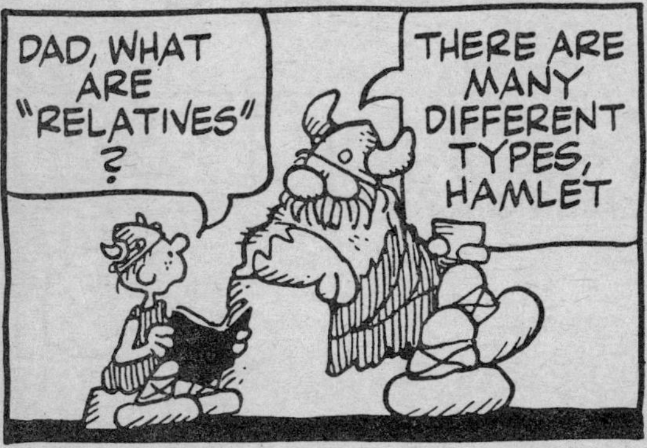
DAD, WHAT ARE "RELATIVES" ?
THERE ARE MANY DIFFERENT TYPES, HAMLET

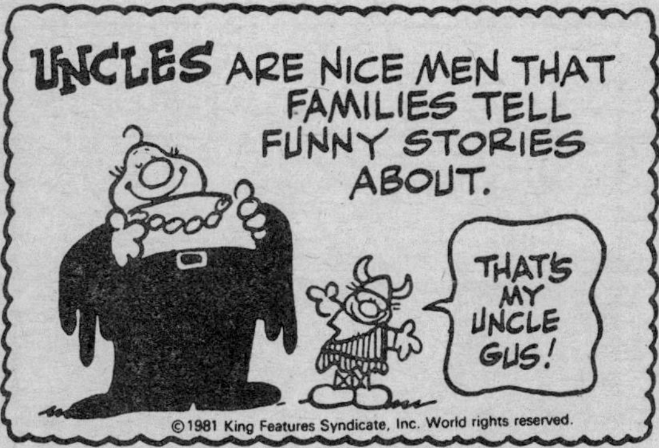
UNCLES ARE NICE MEN THAT FAMILIES TELL FUNNY STORIES ABOUT.
THAT'S MY UNCLE GUS!

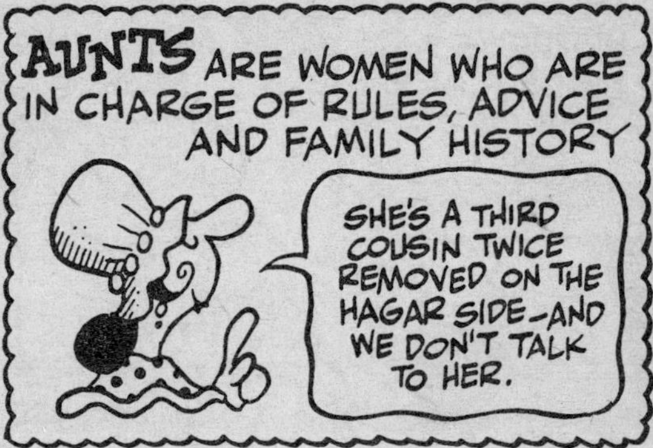
AUNTS ARE WOMEN WHO ARE IN CHARGE OF RULES, ADVICE AND FAMILY HISTORY
SHE'S A THIRD COUSIN TWICE REMOVED ON THE HAGAR SIDE-AND WE DON'T TALK TO HER.

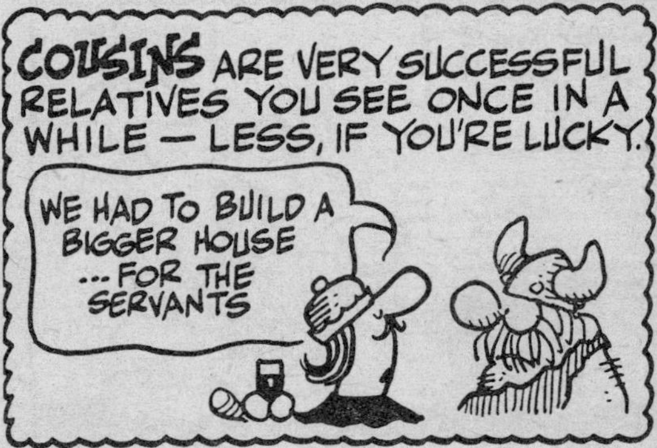
COUSINS ARE VERY SUCCESSFUL RELATIVES YOU SEE ONCE IN A WHILE — LESS, IF YOU'RE LUCKY.
WE HAD TO BUILD A BIGGER HOUSE ... FOR THE SERVANTS

NEPHEWS AND NIECES ARE THE SAME, ONLY YOUNGER...
ANYTHING ELSE?
WHAT ARE "IN-LAWS"?
DON'T ASK
DIK BROWNE
4-5

The End

SNEAKY PETE

IS IT FUN BEING A VIKING, DAD ?
IT'S A LOT OF FUN!
BUT YOU GOTTA BE SMART!

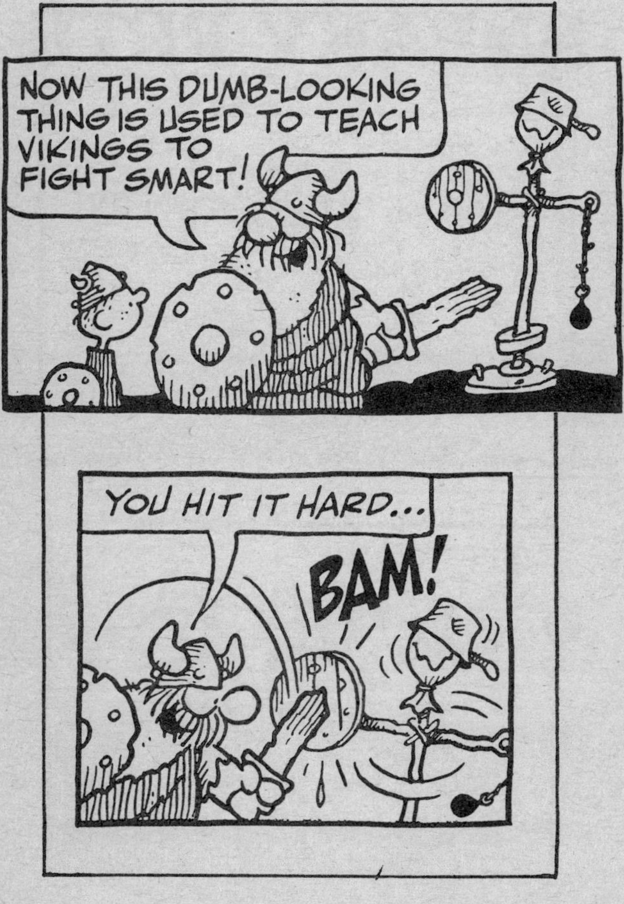
NOW THIS DUMB-LOOKING THING IS USED TO TEACH VIKINGS TO FIGHT SMART!
YOU HIT IT HARD...
BAM!

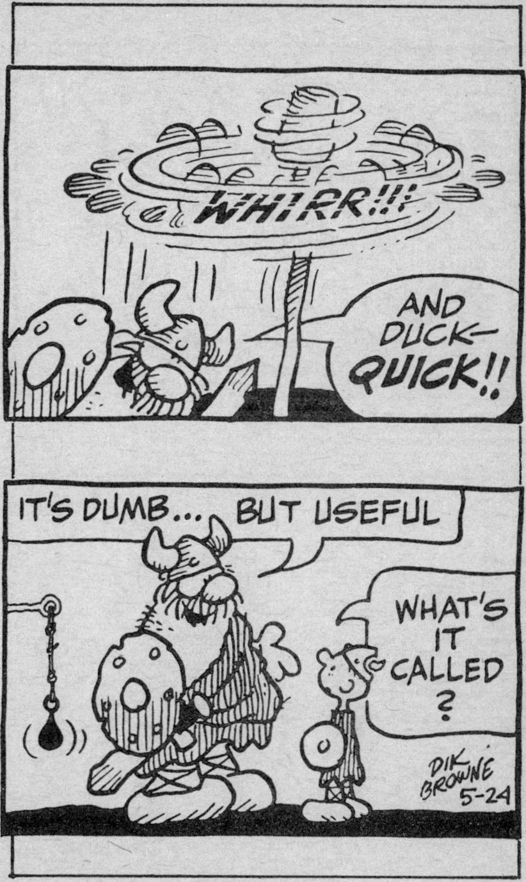
WHIRR!!!
AND DUCK— QUICK!!
IT'S DUMB... BUT USEFUL
WHAT'S IT CALLED ?
DIK BROWNE 5-24

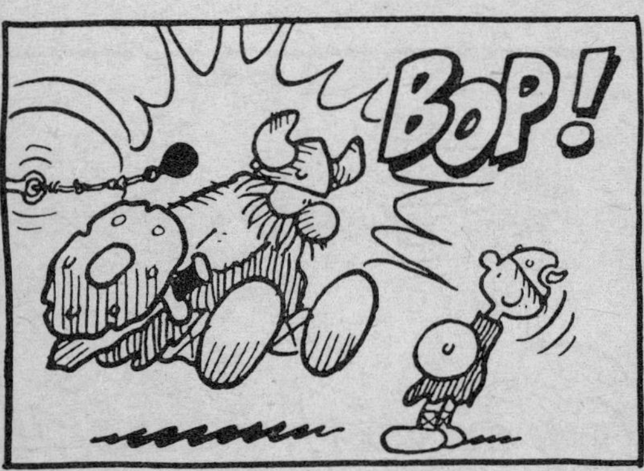
BOP!

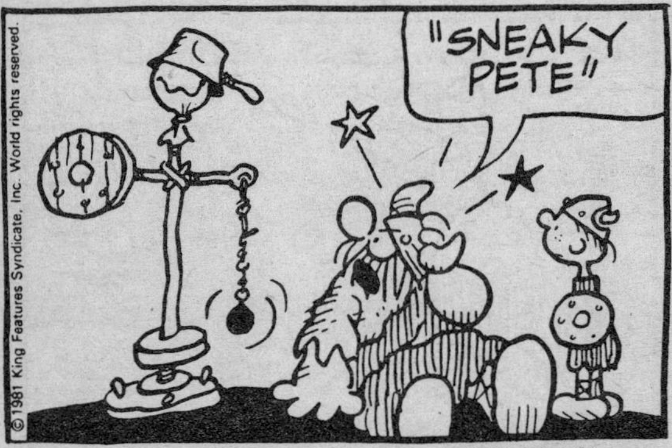
"SNEAKY PETE"
© 1981 King Features Syndicate, Inc. World rights reserved.

The End

PRINCE CHARMING

WHAT'S WRONG WITH HONI ?
NOTHING A MERE MAN WOULD UNDERSTAND
SIGH
...IT'S CALLED "LOVE"

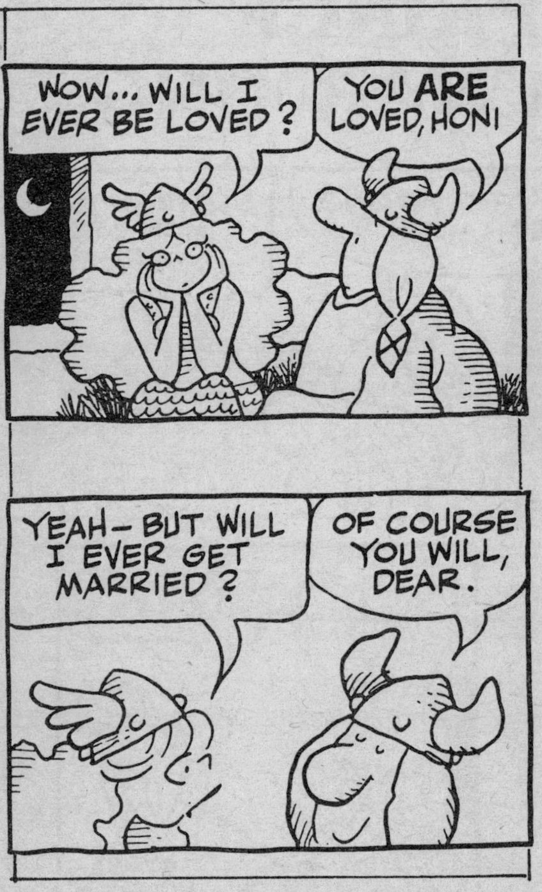
WOW... WILL I EVER BE LOVED?
YOU ARE LOVED, HON!
YEAH– BUT WILL I EVER GET MARRIED?
OF COURSE YOU WILL, DEAR.

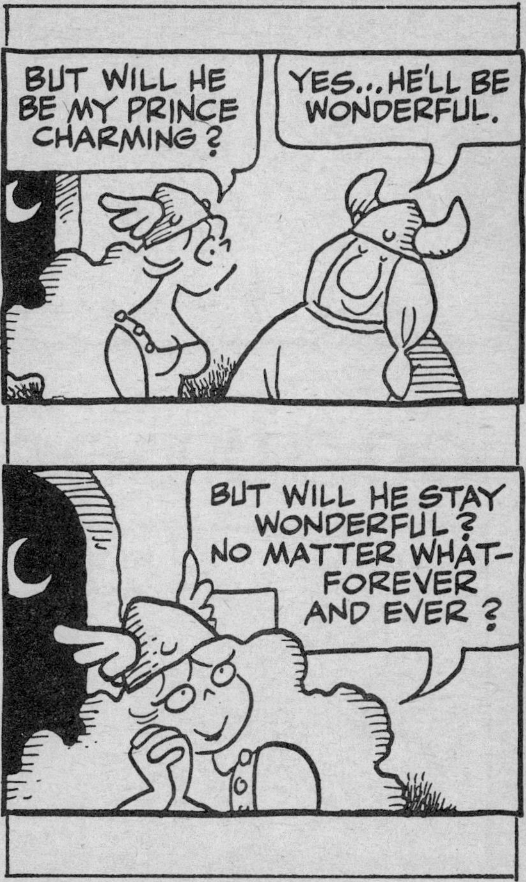
BUT WILL HE BE MY PRINCE CHARMING?
YES...HE'LL BE WONDERFUL.
BUT WILL HE STAY WONDERFUL? NO MATTER WHAT- FOREVER AND EVER?

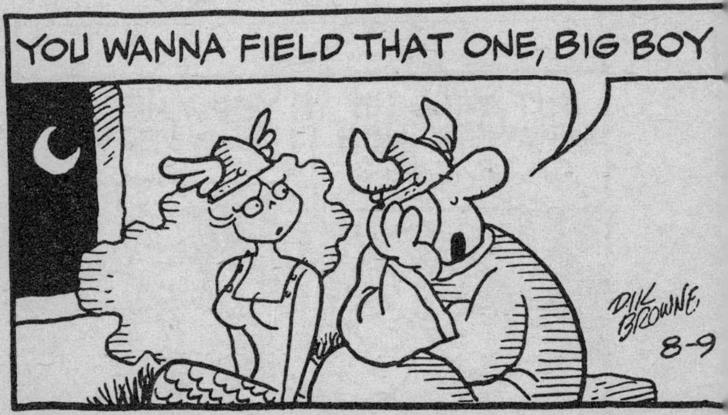
YOU WANNA FIELD THAT ONE, BIG BOY
DIK BROWNE
8-9

GOOD DOG

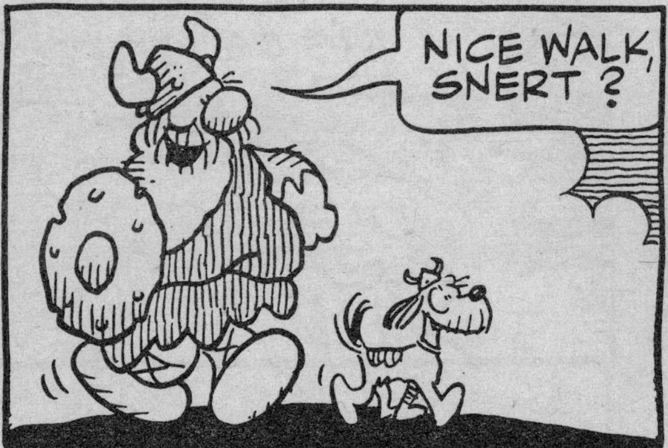
NICE WALK, SNERT ?

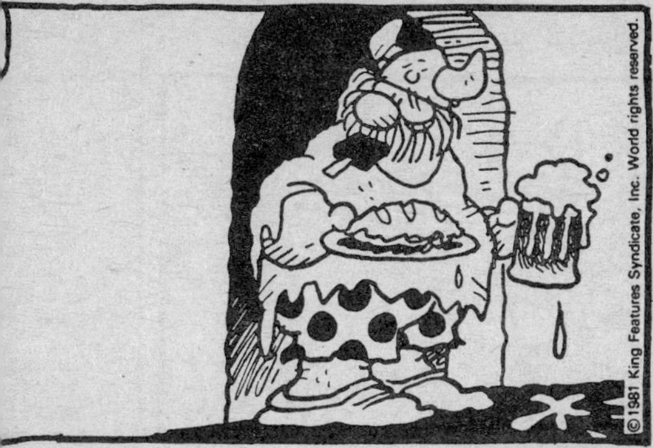

©1981 King Features Syndicate, Inc. World rights reserved.

The End

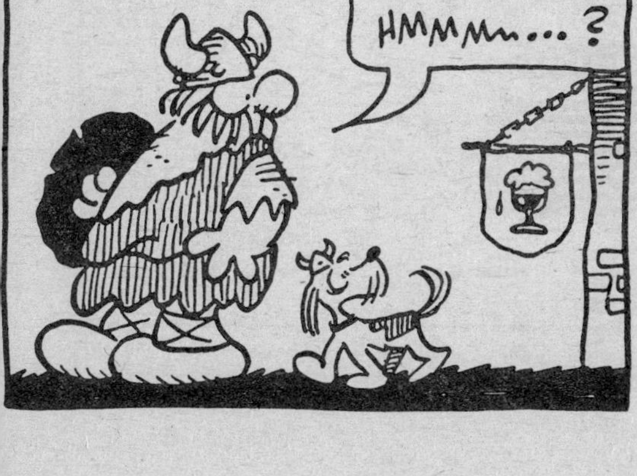

HMMMm... ?

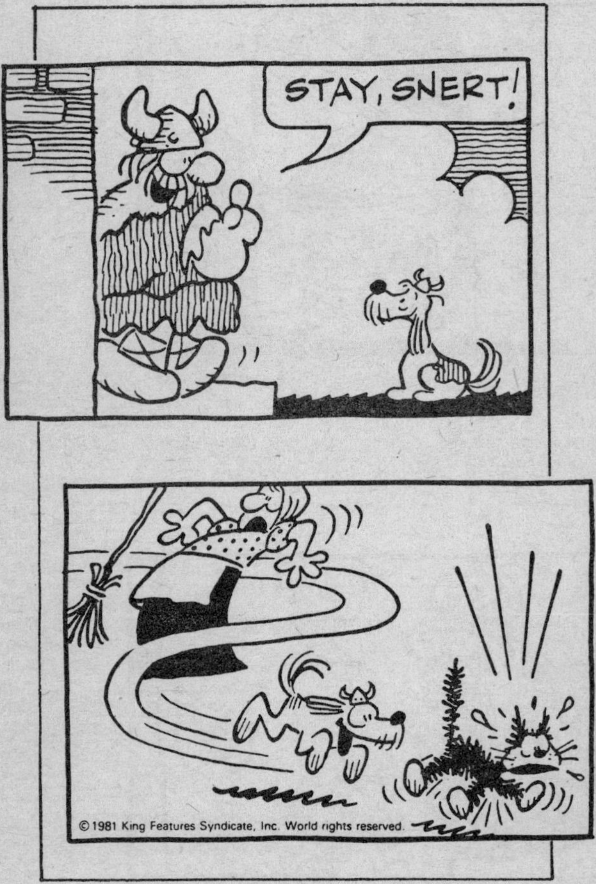
STAY, SNERT!
© 1981 King Features Syndicate, Inc. World rights reserved.

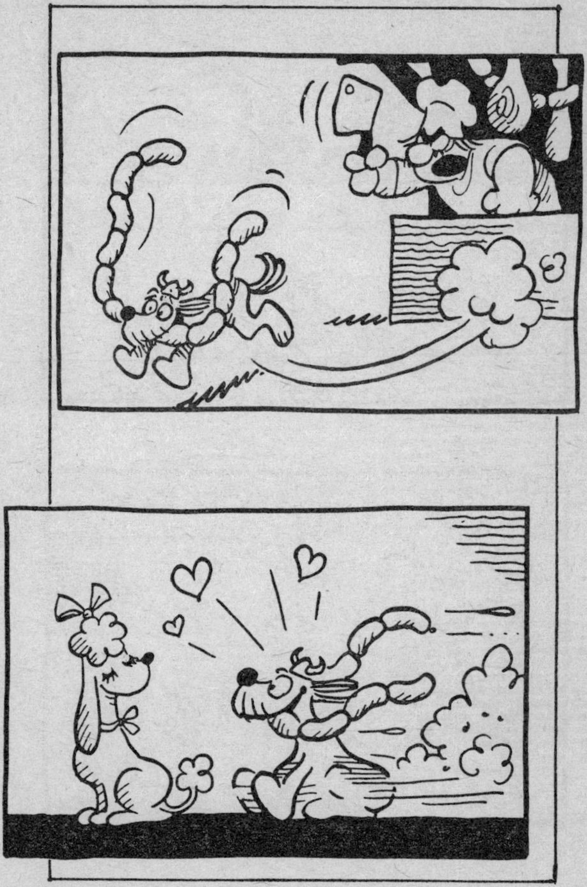

9-20
GOOD DOG!
DIK BROWNE

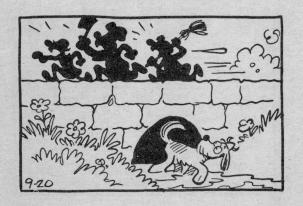

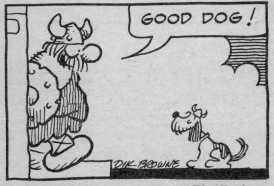

The End

SWORD PLAY

HAMLET, WHAT IS PAPA HOLDING?
PAPA'S BEST SWORD
GOOD! TODAY I TEACH YOU HOW TO USE IT!

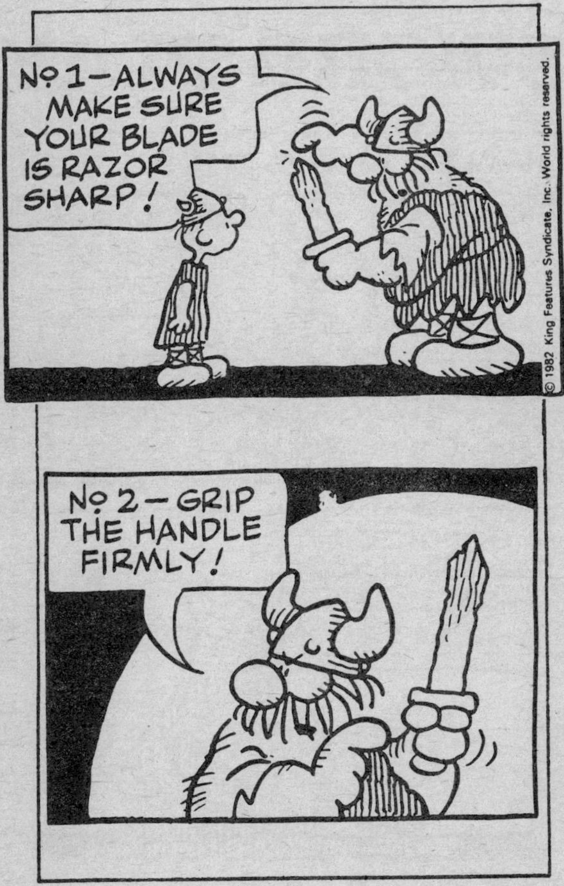
No 1—ALWAYS MAKE SURE YOUR BLADE IS RAZOR SHARP!
© 1982 King Features Syndicate, Inc. World rights reserved.
No 2—GRIP THE HANDLE FIRMLY!

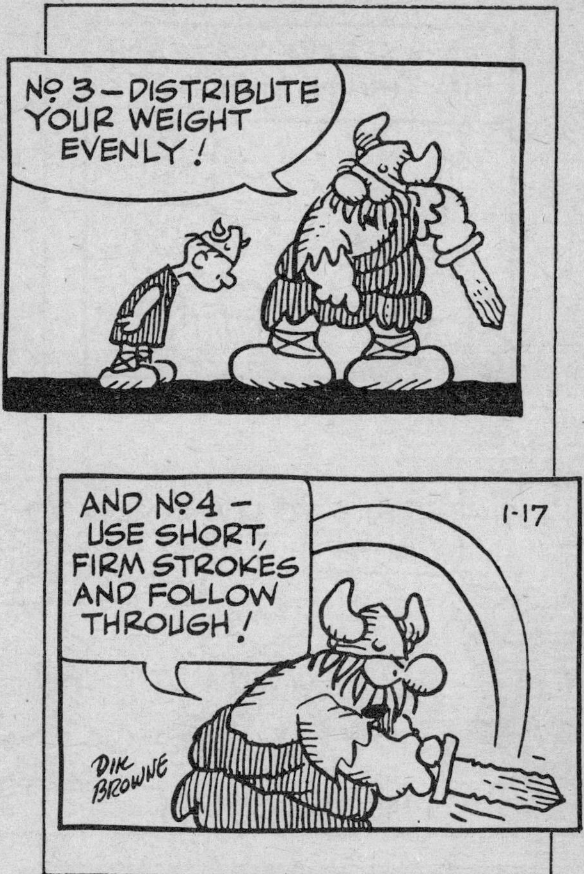
NO. 3 – DISTRIBUTE YOUR WEIGHT EVENLY!
AND NO. 4 – USE SHORT, FIRM STROKES AND FOLLOW THROUGH!
1-17
DIK BROWNE

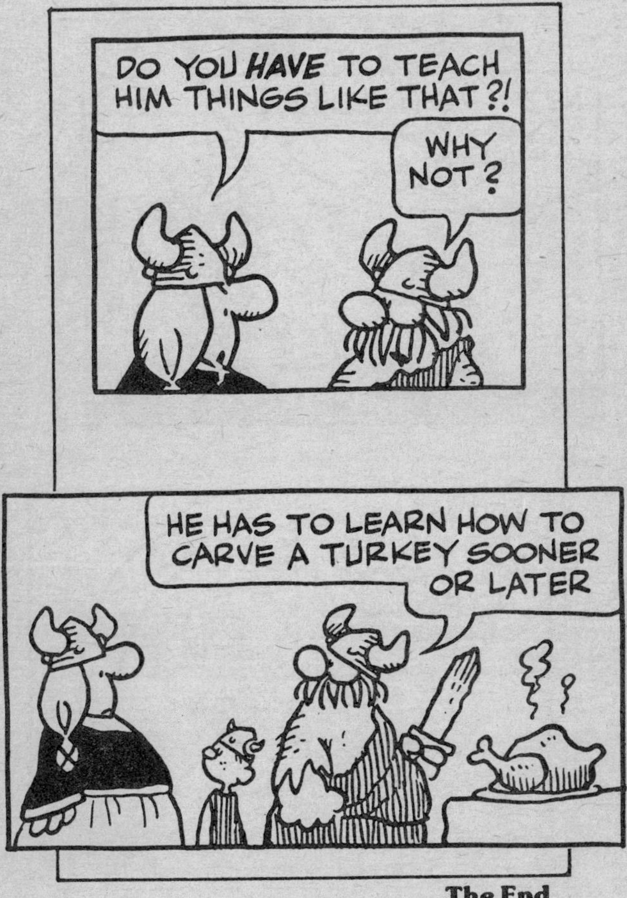
DO YOU HAVE TO TEACH HIM THINGS LIKE THAT?!
WHY NOT?
HE HAS TO LEARN HOW TO CARVE A TURKEY SOONER OR LATER

The End

SAY "NO"!

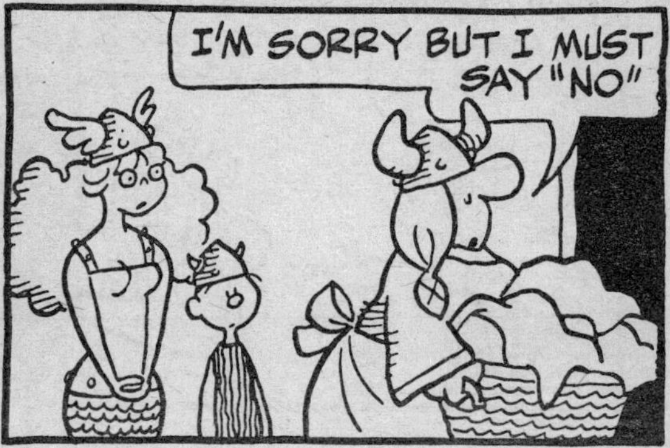
I'M SORRY BUT I MUST SAY "NO"

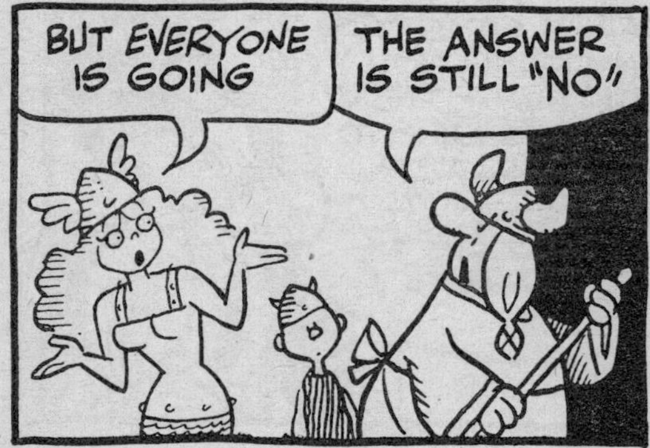
BUT *EVERYONE* IS GOING
THE ANSWER IS STILL "NO"

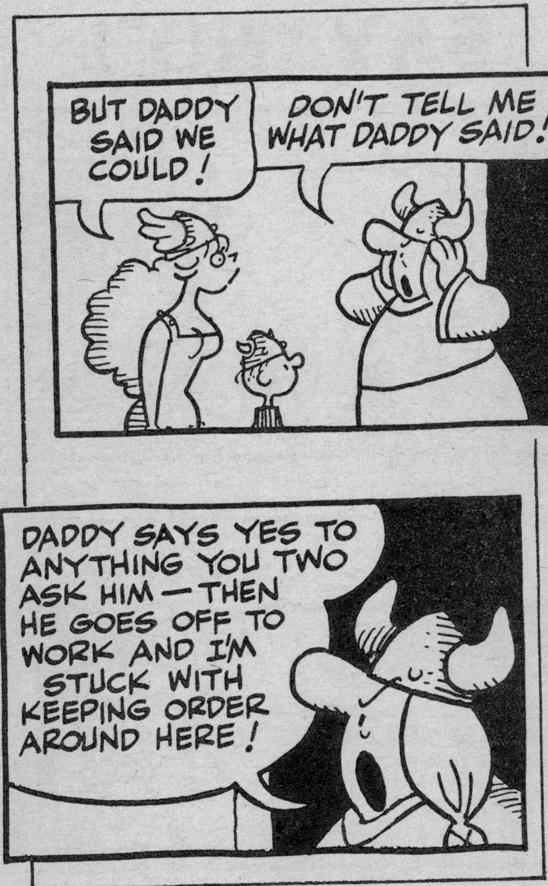
BUT DADDY SAID WE COULD!
DON'T TELL ME WHAT DADDY SAID!
DADDY SAYS YES TO ANYTHING YOU TWO ASK HIM — THEN HE GOES OFF TO WORK AND I'M STUCK WITH KEEPING ORDER AROUND HERE!

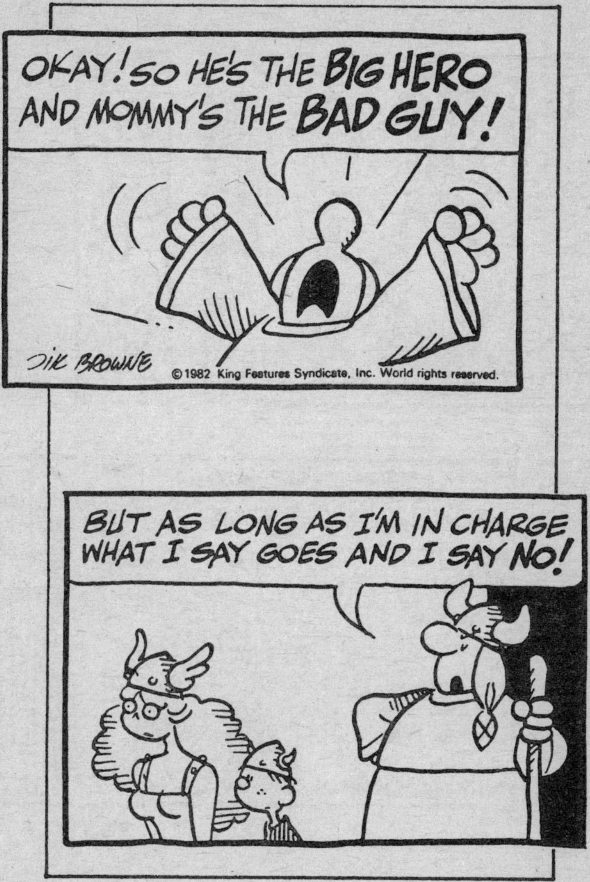
OKAY! SO HE'S THE BIG HERO AND MOMMY'S THE BAD GUY!
DIK BROWNE
©1982 King Features Syndicate, Inc. World rights reserved.
BUT AS LONG AS I'M IN CHARGE WHAT I SAY GOES AND I SAY NO!

HI, HONEY... I'M HOME
3-14
SLAM!!
IT MUST HAVE BEEN SOMETHING I SAID...

The End

VIKING DOG

SNERT! ARE YOU GONNA SLEEP AND LAZE AROUND ALL DAY ?
YOU'LL NEVER BE A VIKING DOG THAT WAY

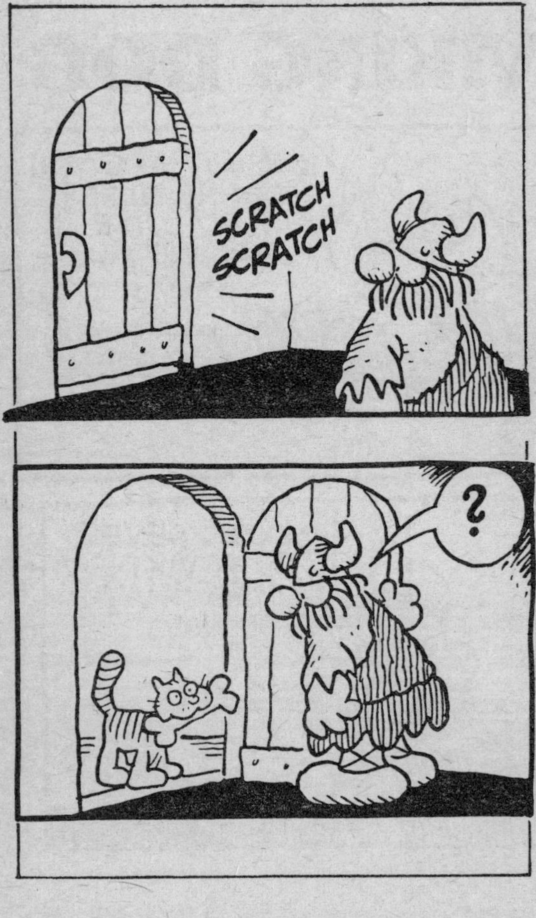
SCRATCH
SCRATCH
?

PLOP!

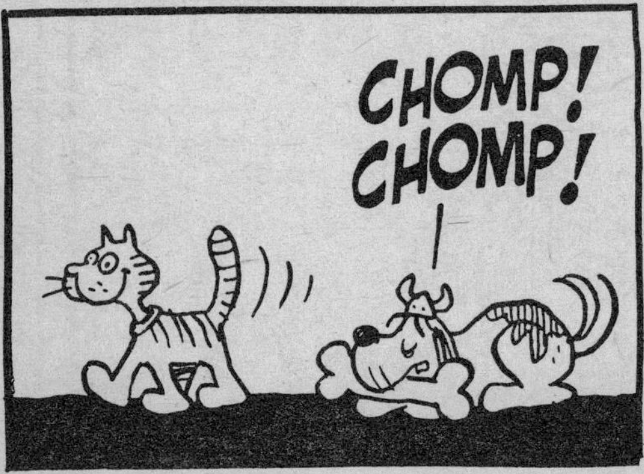
CHOMP! CHOMP!

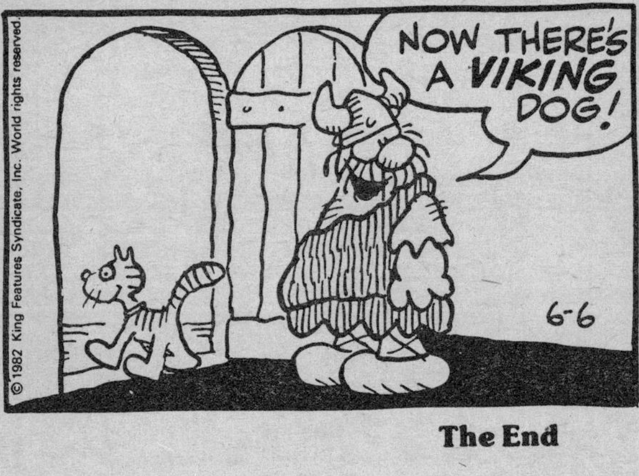
NOW THERE'S A VIKING DOG!
6-6
©1982 King Features Syndicate, Inc. World rights reserved.

The End

THE TRUTH

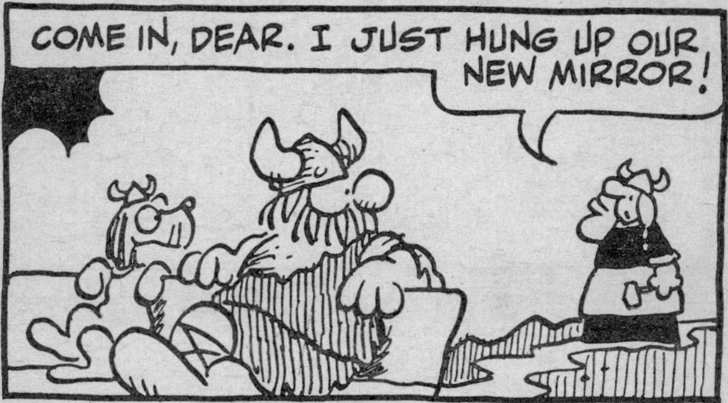
COME IN, DEAR. I JUST HUNG UP OUR NEW MIRROR!

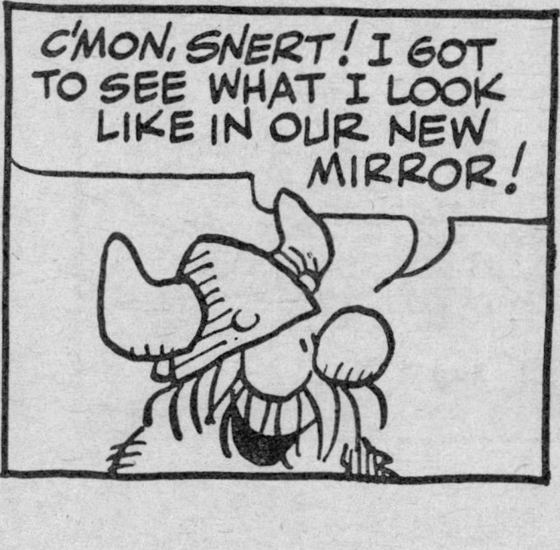
C'MON, SNERT! I GOT TO SEE WHAT I LOOK LIKE IN OUR NEW MIRROR!

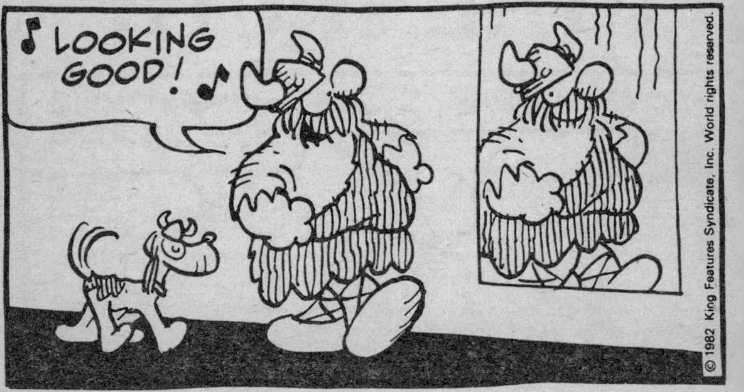
♪ LOOKING GOOD! ♪

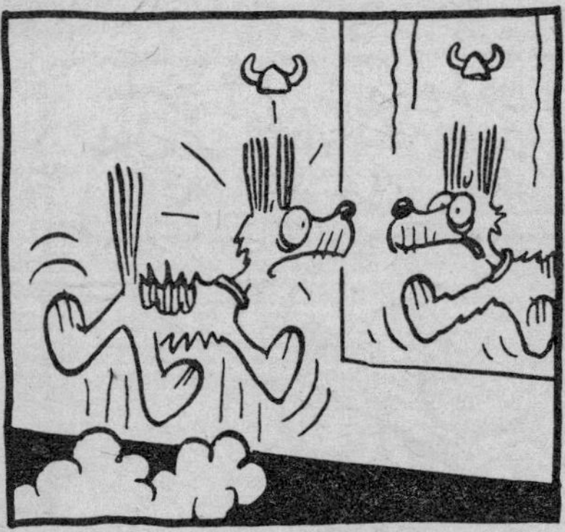

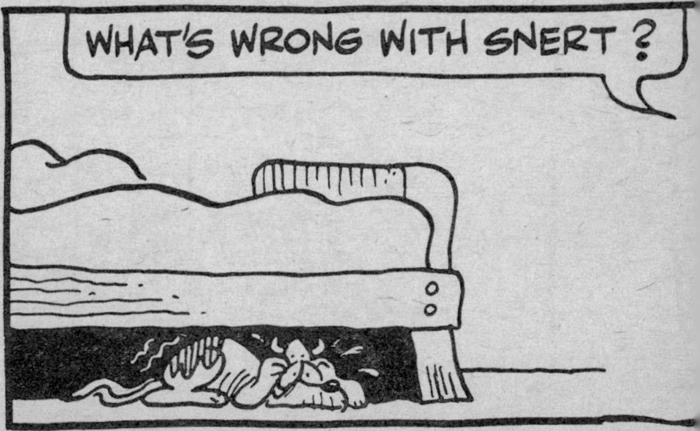
WHAT'S WRONG WITH SNERT?

PLAY DEAD

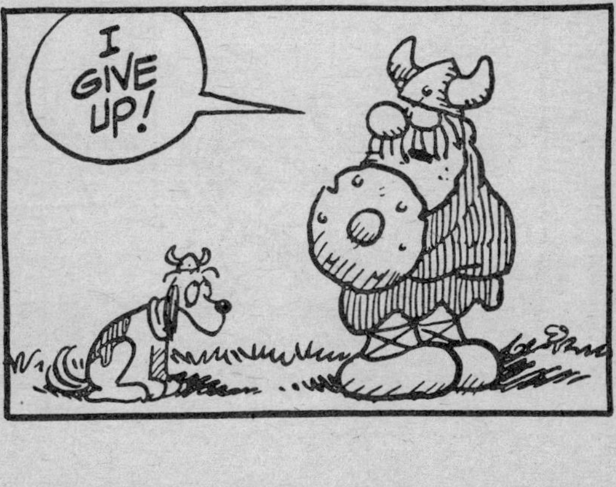
I GIVE UP!

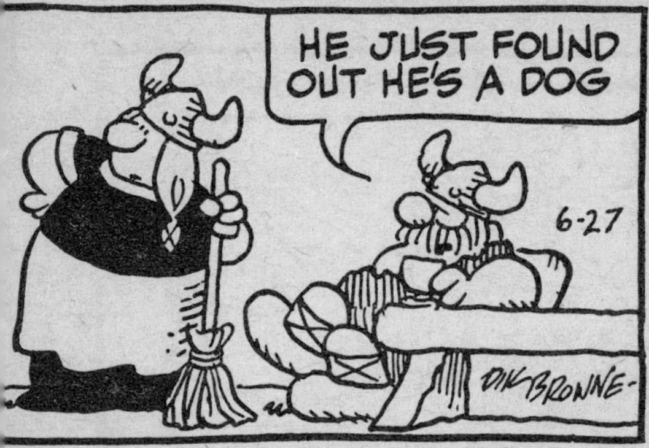
HE JUST FOUND OUT HE'S A DOG
6-27
DIK BROWNE

The End

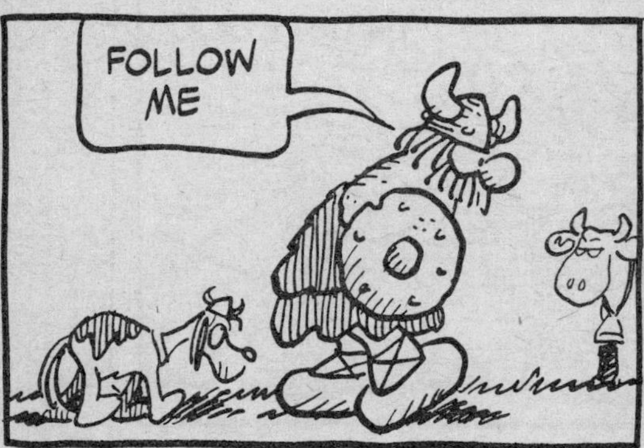
FOLLOW ME

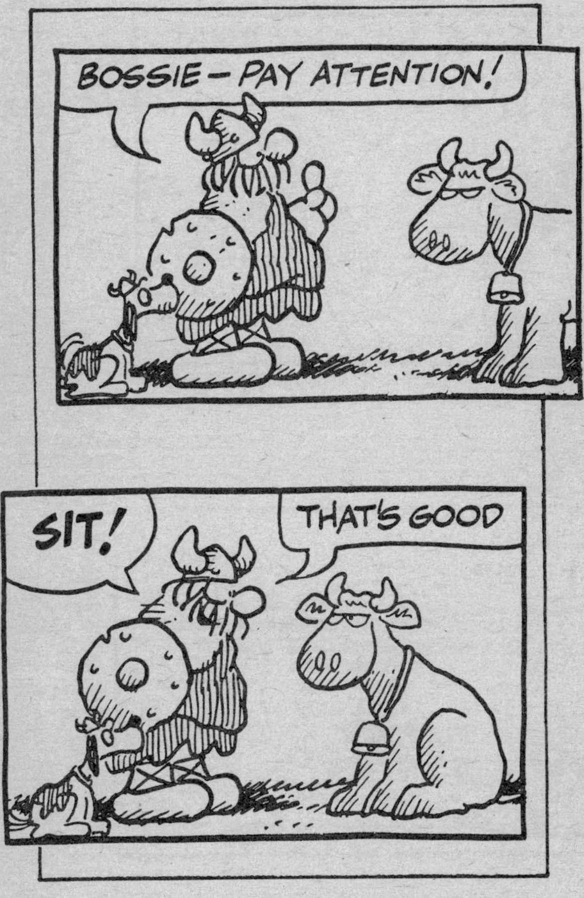
BOSSIE—PAY ATTENTION!
SIT!
THAT'S GOOD

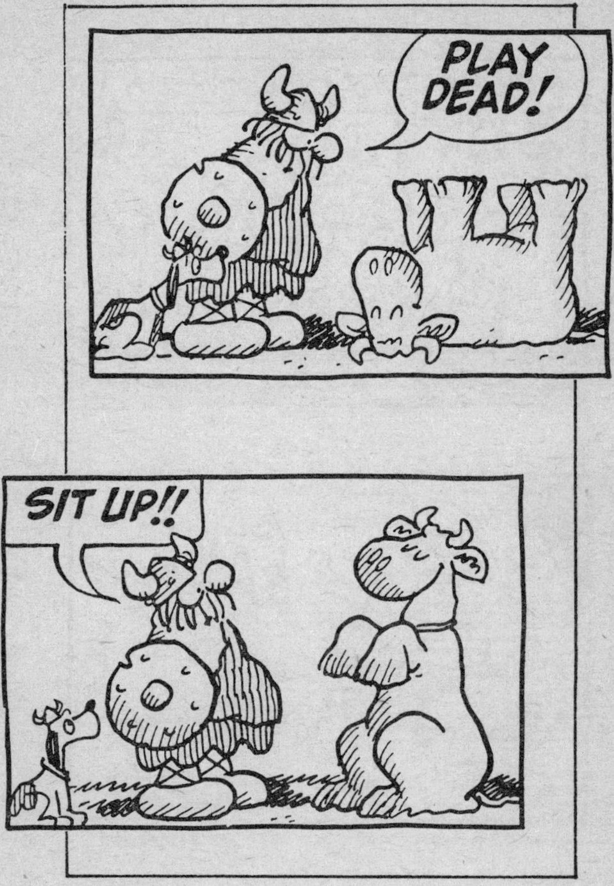
PLAY DEAD!
SIT UP!!

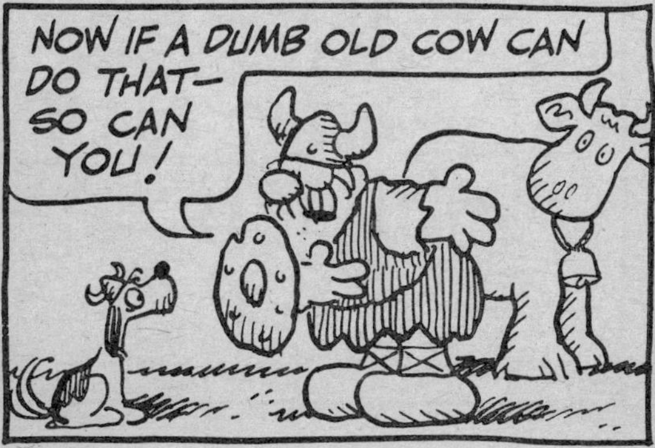
NOW IF A DUMB OLD COW CAN DO THAT— SO CAN YOU!

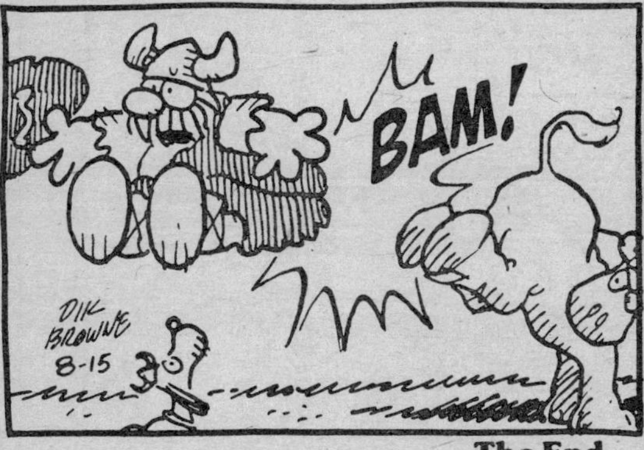
BAM!
DIK BROWNE 8-15

The End

ATHEIST

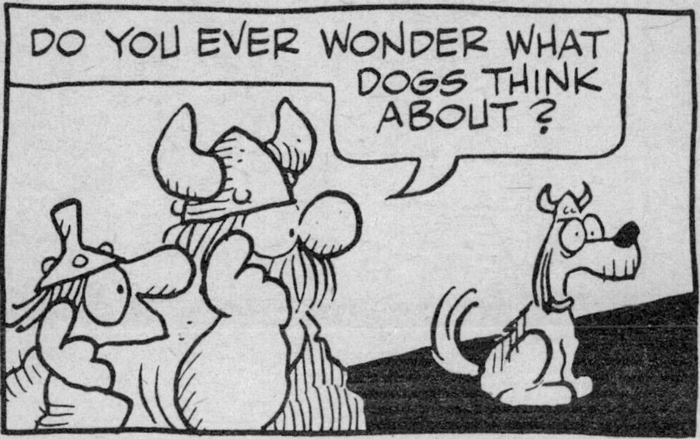
DO YOU EVER WONDER WHAT DOGS THINK ABOUT?

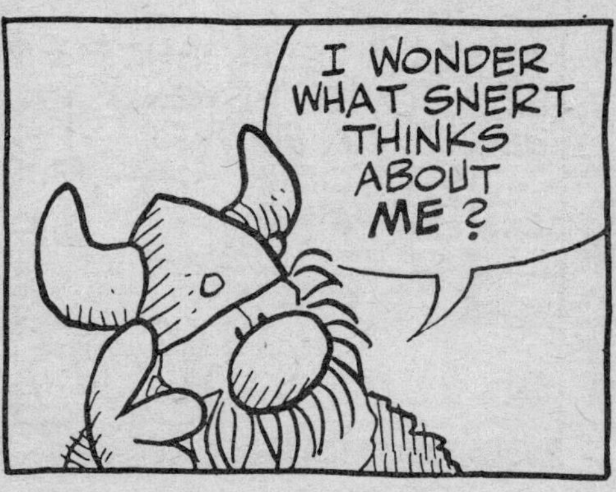
I WONDER WHAT SNERT THINKS ABOUT ME?

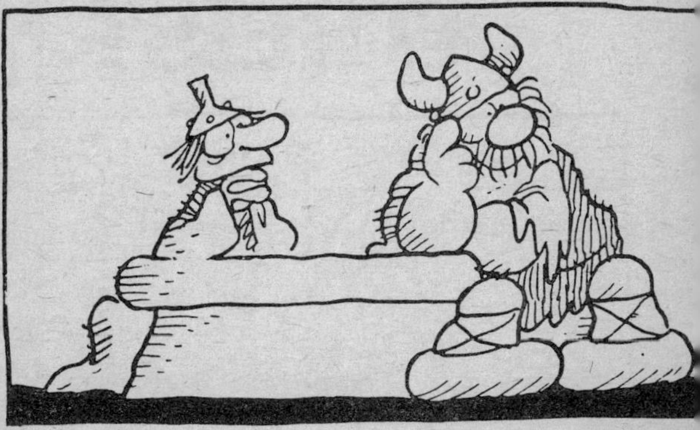

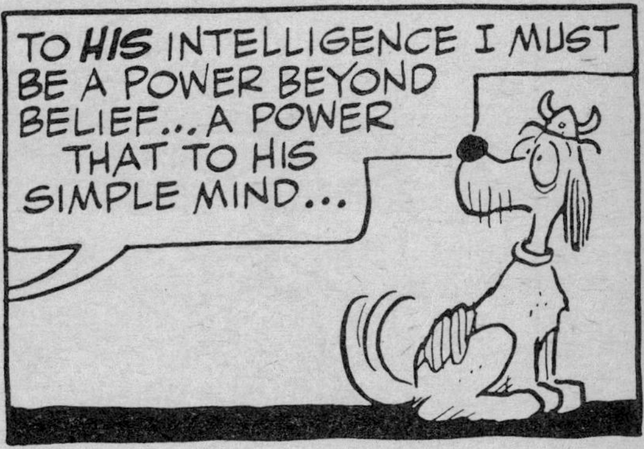
TO HIS INTELLIGENCE I MUST BE A POWER BEYOND BELIEF... A POWER THAT TO HIS SIMPLE MIND...

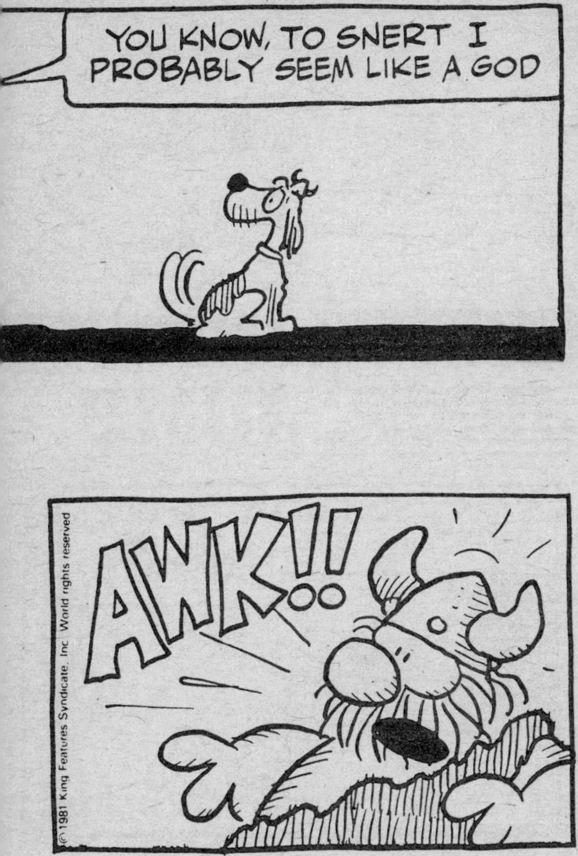
YOU KNOW, TO SNERT I PROBABLY SEEM LIKE A GOD
AWK!!
© 1981 King Features Syndicate, Inc. World rights reserved

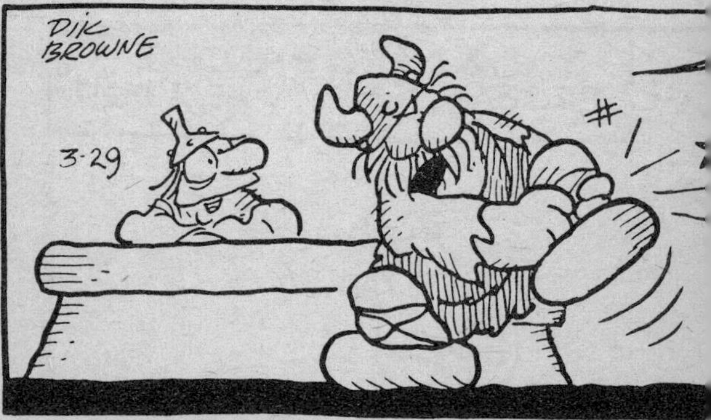
DIK BROWNE
3-29
#

JUMP, JUMP

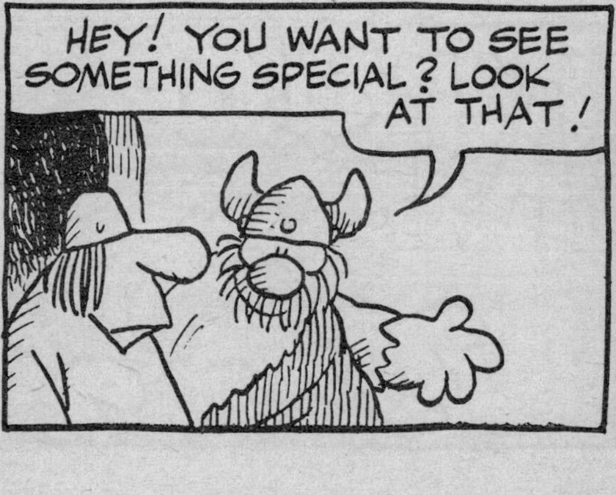
HEY! YOU WANT TO SEE SOMETHING SPECIAL? LOOK AT THAT!

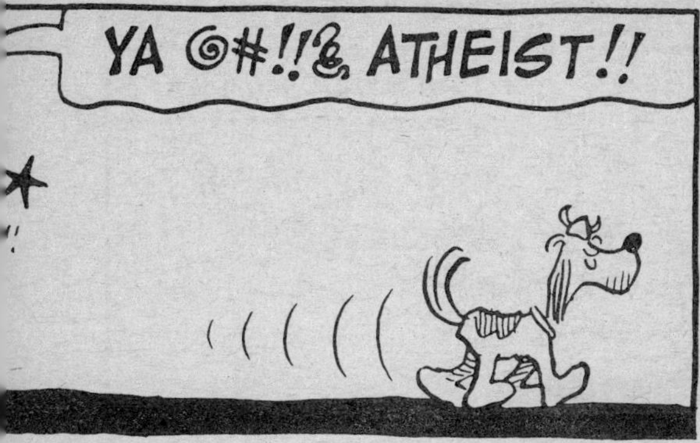
YA @#!!&, ATHEIST!!

The End

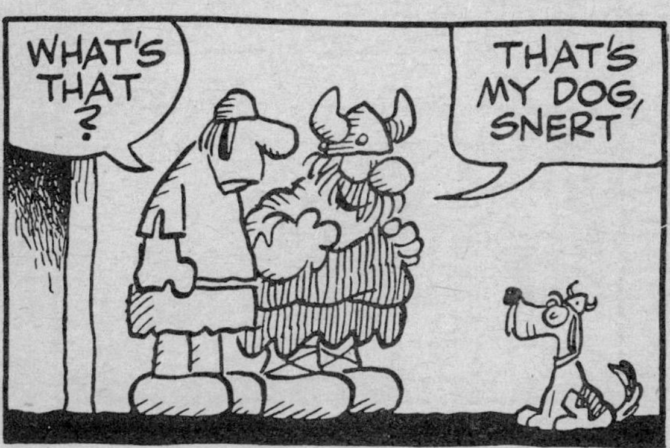
WHAT'S THAT?
THAT'S MY DOG, SNERT

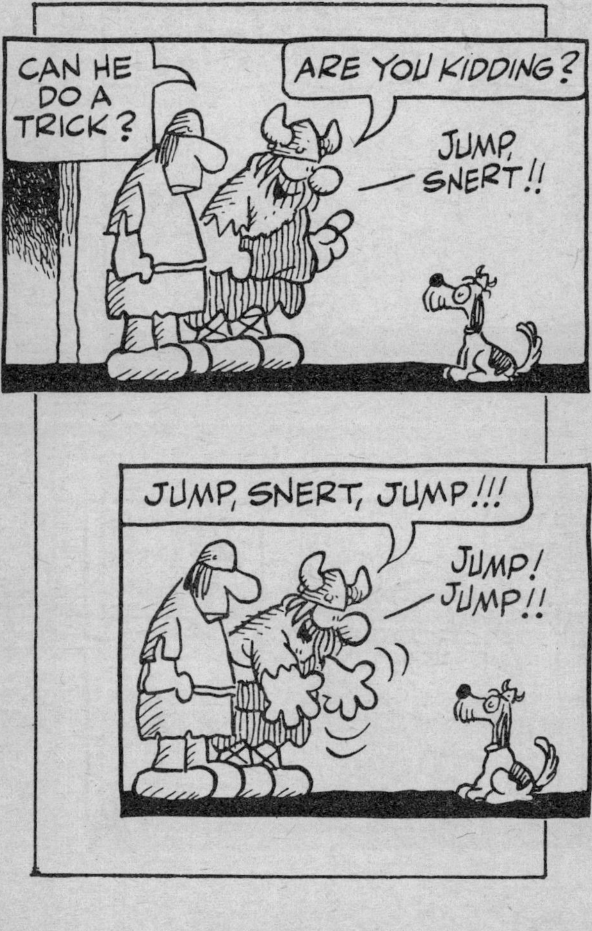
CAN HE DO A TRICK?
ARE YOU KIDDING?
JUMP, SNERT!!
JUMP, SNERT, JUMP!!!
JUMP! JUMP!!

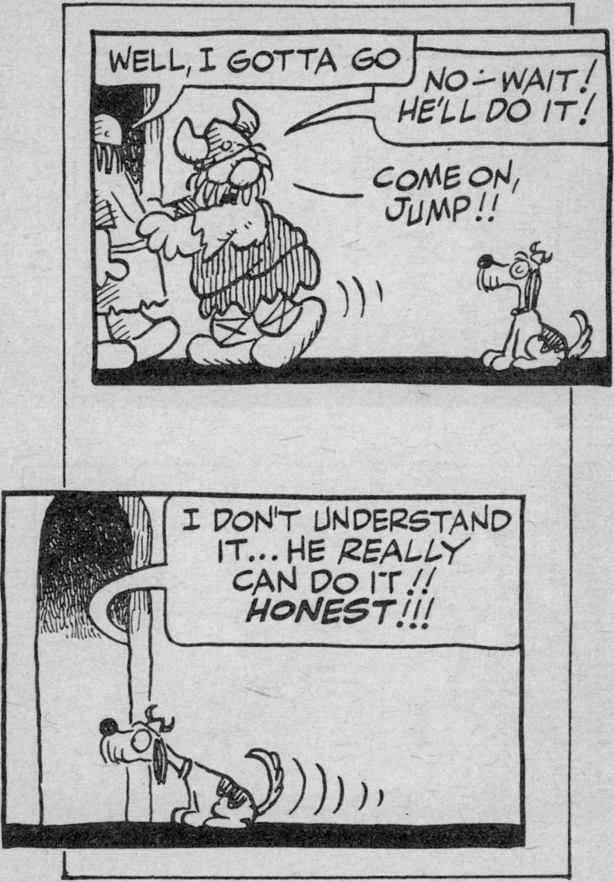
WELL, I GOTTA GO
NO-WAIT! HE'LL DO IT!
COME ON, JUMP!!
I DON'T UNDERSTAND IT... HE *REALLY* CAN DO IT!! **HONEST!!!**

BOING!
© 1981 King Features Syndicate, Inc. World rights reserved.
WAIT TILL YOU WANT SOMEONE TO PLAY "CHASE THE STICK" WITH!
DIK BROWNE 1-18

The End

SAPSUCKER

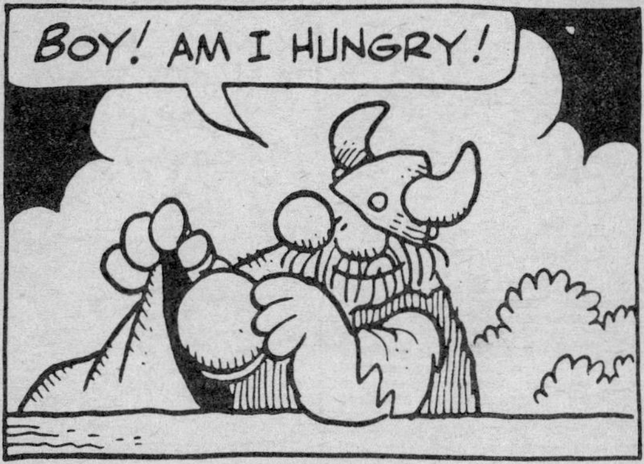
BOY! AM I HUNGRY!

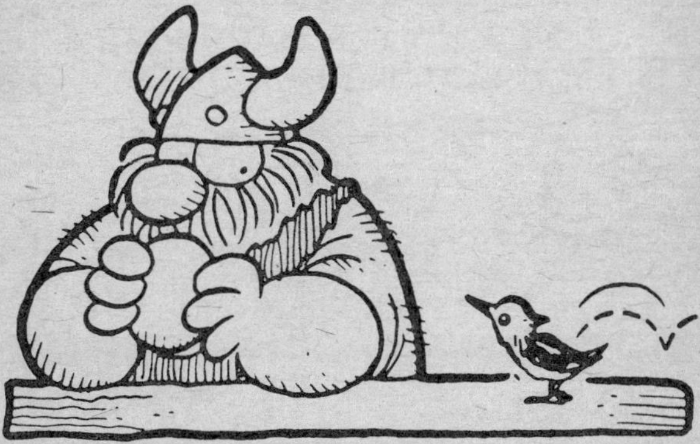

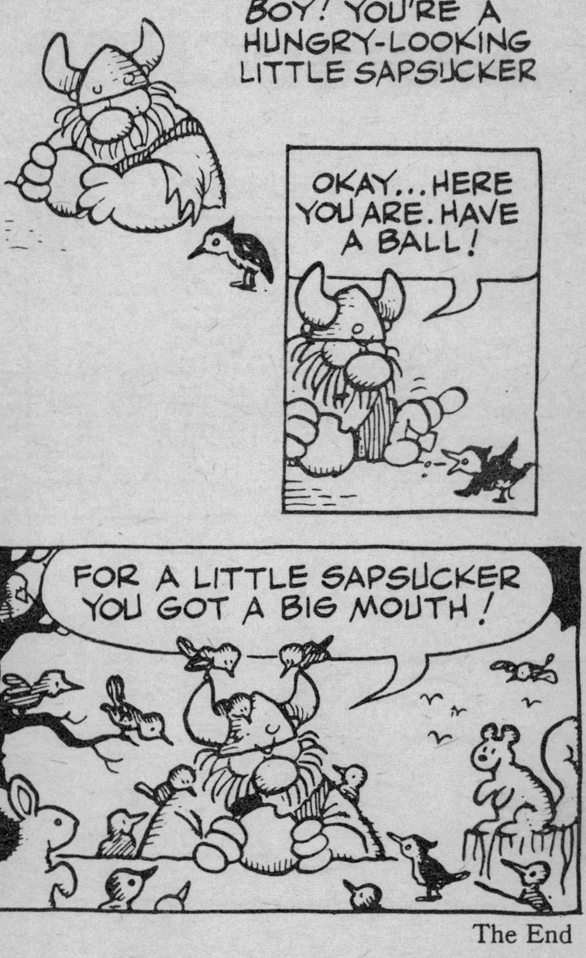
BOY! YOU'RE A HUNGRY-LOOKING LITTLE SAPSUCKER
OKAY...HERE YOU ARE. HAVE A BALL!
FOR A LITTLE SAPSUCKER YOU GOT A BIG MOUTH!

The End